SAVING ELENA

PJ FIALA

DEDICATION

I've had so many wonderful people come into my life and I want you all to know how much I appreciate it. From each and every reader who takes the time out of their days to read my stories and leave reviews, thank you.

My beautiful, smart and fun Road Queens, who play games with me, post fun memes, keep the conversation rolling and help me create these captivating characters, places, businesses and more. Thank you ladies for your ideas, support and love.

The following characters and places were created by:

Nicky Ortiz - **GHOST Headquarters** - The HOG (Home, Office and Garage)

House name ideas

Amy Ball - The Stitchery

Deb Jones Diem - Hemmed In

Kerry Harteker - Mending Box

Karen Cranford LeBeau - Button Down

Julia Murphy - Zipped Tight

Gail Whitley - Needle Point

Dana Zamora - Sown Home

People:
Liz Bradley - Maria Bradley
Tjuana TJ Brown - Shianne Brown
Lyne Carroll & Belinda Jackson Hercule -Elena Dorsey
Cathy Christmas – Helissa
Terri DeMario - Flynn DeMario
Anna Marie Flamini - Amelia
Kerry Harteker - Elena's mom's health issues
Belinda Jackson Hercule - Sharon Jackson
Ginna Honeycutt - Carter Gordon
Kristi Hombs Kopydlowski - Lara Bennit
Kristi Hombs Kopydlowski - Troy Brown
Karen Cranford LeBeau - Klaire Brown
Karen Cranford LeBeau - Aidyn Dunbar
Karen Cranford LeBeau - Millie LeBeau
Sheriff Rex Cranford - Karen Cranford LeBeau
Elinda Moody - Keaton Bennit
Terra Oenning - Rayleigh Winters
Nicky Ortiz - Explosives Expert from Brookswood - Dylan
Pamela Reveal - Matthew Vickers
Yolanda Tobiasen - Laylah Bennit
Jo West - Baxter Fenshaw
Jessica Zoe - Grace Dorsey

Places:
Amy Barber - Fort Abraham
Kim Kurtz - Glen Hollow
Kathy Franklin - Hickory Hills
Monique Mousseau Westwood - Brookswood

Glen Hollow businesses -

Abigail Capps - Paxton's General Store
Nancy Hoch - Homemade in the Hollow
Nathalie Juergensen - Barbershop - Hairy Beards
Nathalie Juergensen - The Broken Barrel
Beckie Johnson Lowe - Chestnut Grove
Nicky Ortiz - Divine Designs
Nicky Ortiz - Porter's Steakhouse
Anne Walker - Lara's Delights
Jo West - Bloomin' Lovely

Black Road Resistance (BRR)
Jamie Rogers - BRR Black Road Resistance
Ronda Barnes-Howard - Everett Howard
Jayne Smith - Craig Howard
Marlene Davis - Hanalore Howard
Sally Harris - Brock Harris
Ginna Honeycutt - Cole Honeycutt
Lynne Kerr - Gerard Weston
Karen Cranford LeBeau - Brenner Matthews
Karen Cranford LeBeau - Ramsey Stewart
Beckie Johnson Lowe - Brayden Lowe
Lisa Mansfield - Reece Mansfield
Mary Lou Melzer - Kent Bennit
Arlene Miklovic - Liliana Weston
Julie Ann Price - Liam Price
Jayne Smith - Theresa
Jo West - Jasiah Weston
Debbie Zsidai - Medicine Woman - Elenor

Last but not least, my family for the love and sacrifices
they have made and continue to make to help me achieve
this dream, especially my husband and best friend, Gene.
Words can never express how much you mean to me.

To our veterans and current serving members of our armed forces, police and fire departments, thank you ladies and gentlemen for your hard work and sacrifices; it's with gratitude and thankfulness that I mention you in this forward.

GLOSSARY - GHOST LEGACY

The kids from GHOST are all grown up and living lives of their own. Meet these men and women of GHOST Legacy:

Tate Vickers - Tate is the son of Gaige and Sophie Vickers. Their story is told in Defending Sophie. Tate is a recon specialist and runs the GHOST satellite office.

Aidyn Dunbar - Is the son of Bridget and Axel Dunbar. You can find their story is Defending Bridget. Aidyn's specialty is sharpshooter and recon.

Spencer Lawson - Spencer is the son of Wyatt and Yvette Lawson. You can read their story in Defending Yvette. Spencer specialize's in security, recon and recovery.

Henry Delany - Henry is the son of Hawk and Roxanne Delany. Their story is told is Defending Roxanne. His specialties are recon, recovery, and anything that requires size.

Adelaide Masters - Adelaide's parents are Josh and Isabella Masters. Their story is told in Defending Isabella. Adelaide served in the Army and is the team's medic.

Maya Sager - Maya served in the US Marine Corps.

Her parents are Dodge and Jax Sager. Their story is told in Finding His Jewel. Maya's specialty is recon and rescue.

Myles Sager - Myles served in the US Marine Corps. Myles and Maya are the twins of Dodge and Jax Sager. Myles is an explosives expert.

DESCRIPTION

GHOST: Government Hidden Ops Specialty Team. They eliminate the threat when no one else can.

He's a GHOST operative wanted for murder.

She's the only resident who can cook up the life-saving elixir that saves her people.

Together they're caught between two worlds embroiled in a raging war.

Aidyn Dunbar killed the leader of Hickory Hills. A necessary move to save the life of his close friend and teammate, but it's placed a bullseye on his chest. Still, he's determined to gather the intel GHOST needs to stop the deadly attacks brought to his adopted home of Glen Hollow, Kentucky.

Elena Dorsey was born and raised in Hickory Hills but has started to see the peaceful way of life she enjoyed as a child turn to greed and destruction. Having no formal education, she struggles to support herself, and her frail mother isn't able to work anymore. If she leaves, she'll be ostracized from the only home she's ever known. There's nowhere for her to go. Or is there?

This quiet, strong woman intrigues Aidyn, and as their interest in each other grows, they flirt with danger from each of their respective communities. Elena holds the key to healing millions of people if Aidyn can assist in her escape. But the leaders of Hickory Hills would rather see her dead than take her popular elixir to the very people they've avoided their entire lives.

Aidyn's job is gathering intel on the Hill people, but his life's mission is now Saving Elena.

———

USA Today bestselling author PJ Fiala brings you the GHOST Legacy series—heroes willing to sacrifice everything in service to their country, and for the men and women they love. A novel with no cliffhanger, *no cheating, and a happily-ever-after.*

Let's stay in touch where bots, algorithms and subjective admins don't decide what we see. PJ Fiala's Readers' Club is my newsletter where I promise to only send you content you enjoy! https://www.subscribepage.com/pjfialafm

1

———

Aidyn ran through the brush, ducking under low branches and jumping over downed ones. The heavy footfalls behind him grew louder. Aidyn would be caught if he didn't change direction or pathway.

His breathing grew labored, and he tripped on a branch covered in dead leaves. Catching himself with his hand before falling over, he righted himself and continued running.

He heard the man chasing him fall on the ground with a thud and an "Oof" grunted out as he fell. Not daring to turn around in case it was a trick, Aidyn ran toward the black road that led him up here.

The instant his feet hit the pavement, he picked up speed and made it to the main road in what felt like record time.

He shot across Main Street, to the parking lot of Bloomin' Lovely, the flower shop in town. His truck sat at the corner of the lot, looking like the best thing he'd ever seen. Shoving his hand into his pocket, he pulled his key fob out and unlocked the doors.

He jumped inside and took off without a backward glance.

His breathing still came in spurts and the sweat he'd produced caused his shirt to stick to his back. He'd need a shower soon. But his teammates were waiting for him.

Navigating the first corner that led him out to the old sewing factory on the edge of town, where he was to meet the rest of his team, he kept his pace within the speed limit and heaved out a deep breath.

Flashing lights and a siren sounded behind him. "Shit!"

A glance in his mirror confirmed the officer was after him. He pulled his truck to the edge of the road and turned on his flashers.

He rolled his window down and lay both hands on top of the steering wheel and waited for the officer.

The officer approached his truck. "May I see your driver's license and insurance papers, please?"

Aidyn glanced out his window and realized this was the new cop Glen Hollow had hired to replace Keaton Bennit.

"I need to reach behind and pull my wallet from my back pocket."

"Go ahead."

He reached back and pulled his wallet out, then held it up as he searched for his driver's license.

He handed it out the window to the officer. What was his name? Aidyn glanced at his name badge. It was obscured by his arm.

"I need to reach into my glove box for my registration."

"Nice and slow, Mr. Dunbar."

He nodded and deliberately reached over to grab his insurance papers.

He held them out to the officer, who looked up at him and squinted in the sunlight. "You're one of the GHOST team."

"Yes, sir."

"Did you just run down the hill?"

He didn't put his work face on this morning and before he could think; he rolled his eyes.

"May as well tell the truth, Mr. Dunbar. I saw you run from the hill."

"Yes. I was doing some recon work."

"It looked like you were being chased."

"Yeah, I was being chased."

The officer looked back at the hill, then took a deep breath. Aidyn felt like he used to feel when he was a kid and he'd disappointed his parents. They tried to keep their frustrations hidden, but neither of them managed it. He'd been a bit of a handful through his teen years. He had help being a bit of a shit though. And that help was all here in Glen Hollow, Kentucky. Lord, help them all.

"I know I'm new here. But I've been told no one is to go up the mountain without reason and without letting our office know."

Aidyn rested his elbow on the door of his truck and smiled at Officer Gordon.

"I'm not privy to what you've been told, Officer Gordon." He held his hand out to shake the officer's hand. "It's nice to meet you, by the way."

Officer Gordon nodded. "It's nice to meet you as well, Mr. Dunbar."

"Aidyn."

"Aidyn. My name is Carter."

"Carter. I'm not aware of what you've been told, but I hope some of that was the fact that we work for the

Department of Defense. We know our jobs and are good at them. We don't stop and ask permission before doing them. If we fuck up, the DoD will let us know."

"I have been told that. I've also been told that you shot Everett Howard and you are the last person on this whole earth who is welcome up there."

Aidyn shrugged. "I still have a job to do."

"Right." Carter handed his insurance papers and his driver's license back. He stepped back a couple of feet. "I stopped you because I saw you running down the hill and it looked suspicious. If you were being chased, someone is aware you were up there. I hope we won't have issues because you've upset them."

Aidyn lifted his hands, then let them fall. "If trouble comes knocking, we'll take care of it."

Carter blew out a breath. "Can I be honest with you?"

"Of course."

"I'd like the time to get acclimated here before some nasty shit comes down the pike, or hill. If you know what I mean."

Aidyn pressed his lips together. "I know what you mean. Look, things are shaky right now, but we periodically go up there to make sure they aren't playing with electricity or messing with our power sources. We're just doing our part to keep them from harming us."

Carter stretched his shoulders. "Okay, Aidyn. Thanks for the heads-up and the chat. I guess I've heard all the bad stuff and not enough of the good. I'll keep my imagination in check."

Aidyn grinned and nodded. "Sounds like a brilliant plan. If you don't need anything else from me, my teammates are waiting for me out at the sewing factory."

"Nah, go on, I'm sorry to keep you."

2

E lena entered her cabin and a shiver skittered down her back as the warmth wrapped around her. She glanced to the fireplace in the right corner of her one-room home and saw the need for more wood. Laying her basket on the old wooden table, she rubbed her hands together to warm them. She stooped to pull two logs from the stack in the corner and set them on top of the small fire in the grate. The dried wood began to burn and the sap on the outside cracked and popped as the flames grew. She remembered carrying the stones for the fireplace from around the mountain and stacking them on a pile before her father had turned that pile of rocks into this fireplace.

She moved toward her mother's bed at the far end of the cabin, which wasn't far from the fire. Her father had built this cabin when Elena was ten. Their former cabin had grown too small and one of the men had recently married and traded building help and supplies for their much smaller cabin. This one offered them room for two beds at the back, and a curtain that could be pulled closed to separate the living area from the bedroom. In the winter months they rarely closed the curtains because it blocked the heat.

She looked down at her mom, sleeping, though she looked fitful. Her covers were crumpled and her left foot jutted out of the blankets.

Elena straightened her blankets and gently tucked her foot under them.

Her mom's eyes opened. "Elena. You were gone a long time."

"I'm sorry, Mama. I was having luck gathering bluebells an' some others. I'll be able to propagate many plants this winter."

Her mom's weak smile made her heart flutter. She was growing weaker by the day.

"Is it supper time?" she whispered.

"Soon. I was planning on making soup. I have fresh carrots and potatoes. And Jasiah got a deer this morning and gave me enough to add to the soup."

"That sounds good."

Elena brushed her mom's hair from her eyes and smiled. "Rest a bit. I'll get the soup started."

Her mom's eyes closed again and Elena took a deep breath and began pulling items from her basket.

She'd dug the potatoes from a patch she'd planted earlier in the year. The carrots too, though it was beginning to get too cold for the vegetables to survive. Tomorrow she'd go and pull them all up and put them in the keep alongside their cabin. The temperature wasn't freezing yet. It was in the low forties, but it was still early January and would likely get a bit colder before the weather changed and spring warmed them.

She pulled a pot from the wooden stand under the

counter and carried it to the fireplace. Grabbing the fire poker, she pulled the wrought iron hook from inside, hooked the handle of her kettle on the hook and poured water from the pitcher on the counter into it.

She hummed as she cut her carrots and potatoes and dropped them into the pot. She gathered herbs and spices as she looked for plants and seeds. As she dropped them into the warming soup, the fragrance filled the air. Finally, she added the fresh venison pieces to her soup. Pushing the kettle and hook into the fireplace, she cleaned up.

She added her flowers and seeds to the various canning jars she'd collected and placed them on the wooden shelves her dad had made. Loud voices outside the cabin diverted her attention.

She tiptoed to the door and listened. "I know it was that fucker from town. The one who killed Everett."

"How do you know that?"

"Dark hair and a beard. He was wearing that fucking blue cap he wears with the gun club logo on it."

She closed her eyes. Her stomach tightened. Aidyn had been up here. She thought she heard running while she was on the east side of the mountain, but she didn't see anything. He was going to get himself killed if he kept coming up here. She needed to warn him.

"Keep an eye out. If they come back up here, grab him and bring him up to Craig."

Their footsteps crunched on the gravel outside and faded into the air.

She stirred her soup, then finished sorting her seeds and plants. Tonight, after they ate, she'd slip down the mountain and leave a note for Aidyn.

Her mom sat up in bed and Elena watched as she reached for her shoes and slipped them on. She pulled the blanket from the foot of the bed and wrapped it around her shoulders as she moved into the kitchen.

Elena pulled two of the three bowls they owned from under the sink and set them on the table. She gathered their spoons and filled their bowls with the hot soup.

It smelled wonderful and it would warm them for sure. Eating quietly, she allowed her thoughts to imagine Aidyn sitting here with them. Eating her soup and enjoying it. She'd been enamored with him from the first time she'd seen him. Something about his demeanor. He was sure of himself. He had confidence and vitality. But he was also considerate of others. She'd watched him and his friends from the cover of brush as they worked down on the base. He laughed easily with his friends and his smile was stunning.

"The soup is good, Elena."

Elena jerked slightly. "Thanks, Mama."

"You're lost in thought."

She tried to smile. "I was. Thinking about the best way to divide up some of the plants I found today. I'd like to propagate them differently this year. I think I can grow healthier plants by rooting them in water first rather than drying them out for seeds."

Her mom stopped eating and stared into her eyes. "You can do that." Elena took another spoonful of soup, but her mom didn't stop staring. "I don't think that was what you were thinking of, though."

Her cheeks heated and she swallowed the soup in her mouth.

"Mama."

Her mom shook her head slightly. "You be careful. You're all I've got."

3
___

Aidyn tossed the last of his t-shirts on top of the pile in his suitcase. They'd be in there for a few minutes. Just as long as it took him to get from this house, out to the sewing factory. So he didn't worry about wrinkles or packing appropriately.

He zipped the suitcase closed and set it on the floor. He pulled the strap to his computer case over his shoulder and picked up his suitcase before exiting his room. His teammates' voices could be heard downstairs. They'd worked their asses off getting permits and licenses before finally being able to remodel the sewing factory. Moving in today felt like a victory. A hard fought one at that. Between the BRR breaking windows, the builders and town council, they'd been playing games around this property for months. The BRR had finally stopped breaking things once the wrought iron fence had been installed.

Gaige and Sophie Vickers, Tate's parents, helped them so much. Sophie acted as their project manager, since after all, GHOST was picking up the tab on it all. But, she'd done a spectacular job. Yesterday they'd installed all the remaining security cameras needed. Tonight, hopefully, they'd all sleep better than they had been. The BRR kept them on their toes running up and down the streets at night. Causing trouble at the base. And generally being pains in the ass. With the fencing came large iron gates that opened once a security card was scanned. The BRR could try to climb over the eight-foot-high fence, but they'd be on camera the entire time and then they'd go to jail.

As he stepped into the dining room at the bottom of the steps, Spencer and Maya were finishing up on their computers.

"Everything okay?"

Maya nodded, her ponytail swishing. "Yep. All good. Spencer has all the camera feeds loaded up on all of our computers and all of them are working."

Spencer shrugged and held his hands out before him. "I'm just that good."

Aidyn chuckled. "Modest too."

He sauntered toward the back door and out to his truck. Tate and Lara were outside with Adelaide and Henry listening to someone on the phone.

Henry glanced at him and grinned.

The voice over the phone was none other than Sheriff Cranford. "Carter saw him with his own eyes."

Aidyn's eyes shifted to Tate, who had a slight grin on his face. "As I said Sheriff, we don't need your permission to do our jobs. We'll go up there as often as we need to, to make sure the BRR isn't planning any more of their assaults on us."

"A heads-up would be nice."

"Well, Sheriff, it would be, but then again, we don't

always have the time to give a heads-up and we won't be reduced to having to call every time we have something to investigate."

The sheriff grumbled and the squeak noted he'd shifted in his chair. "Alright. Gotta go."

The call ended and Tate pocketed his phone. "I think Carter is a bit of a scaredy cat."

Henry chuckled. "Can't blame him, sort of. I'm sure all he's hearing are the horrific things that happened. Not how for years there was peace."

Aidyn opened his truck door and laid his computer case on the passenger seat and his suitcase on the floor.

"Yeah, he stopped me on my way to the sewing factory today. He said as much. I told him not to worry. We're good at our jobs and know what we're doing."

Henry chuckled, "Then he went and tattled to the sheriff."

Tate shrugged. "It's good we know his personality. Let's not rely on him for much until he gets his feet wet. The first time the BRR screws with him, he'll be looking for us."

Adelaide giggled. "Pussy."

Tate clapped his hands. "Okay, ready to move?"

Henry turned toward his truck. "Yep. Looking for a good night's sleep."

Adelaide shook her head, "We need a new name. We keep calling it the sewing factory but, it's not that anymore. Can we call it something besides that or the compound?"

Tate grinned. "Suggestions?"

"I don't know. I've been thinking about it. So far nothing clever has come up."

Aidyn chuckled. "Keep thinking. We all can."

He jumped in his truck and watched as his friends did the same. Tate pulled out first. The bullet holes in his truck were finally fixed. It had been the welcome card from hell. At least Tate thought so.

He waited for Henry and Adelaide to pull out before he did. Maya and Spencer were just leaving the house now and loading up their vehicles.

Waving at them he moved out of the driveway and on to their new home.

Dusk was quickly settling in and the weather was cooler now than it had been this morning. Rather than turning left and following his teammates, he headed out toward the main road in front of the mountain. He found more and more the urge to drive along that road to see if he could see Elena moving around. He never could, unless she wanted him to see her. She moved like a mist. She could walk along the woods so quietly it seemed that she floated.

He slowed as he neared the large tree nearest the edge of the road. It was covered with winter creeper, a vine-like plant that eventually smothered out its host tree. But it also offered ground cover and Elena had left him small baskets with notes in them in the past. Now he found himself unable to drive anywhere without looking to see if she'd left him a note. It was purely childish on his part to be excited by anything like this, but he allowed himself the childish pleasure. They dealt with heavy ugly stuff most of the time, this seemed like frivolous fun.

He slowed as the tree came into view and pulled to the edge of the road. Jumping from his truck, he stalked to the edge of the road and peered into the viny coverage. He saw it. A small brown basket handle peering from the top of the vines.

Reaching into the vines for the basket, his heart raced, and his hands shook slightly. He pulled the basket from its hiding spot and practically ran to his truck.

As soon as he was inside, he took off for a safer place to look at what she'd left him. He decided on a spot behind Lara's bakery, since she and Tate were moving into the sewing factory tonight.

He turned down the alley behind the bakery but stopped out of range of her camera. He pulled the basket toward him and lifted the piece of material laying inside. There lay a note on a piece of notebook paper. It was the paper he'd given her. A small five by three-inch pocket notebook and a pen he'd left in the basket for her last week. He'd noticed she had to write notes on whatever she could find so he bought these for her. His heart swelled that she'd used it.

His fingers shook slightly as he unfolded the piece of paper. "Be careful. They'll be watching for you. They want to bring you to Craig if you're caught. E."

4

After leaving her basket under the winter creeper where she'd been leaving notes for Aidyn, she swished along the edge of the mountain to the nearest road so if she was seen, it would look as though she'd come from a different direction. She'd promised her mom she'd be careful, and she would be.

She found some mushrooms she'd hidden just for this purpose and put them in the sack which her mom had made for her many years ago. She took good care of it and only used it when she needed to keep her hands free as it had a strap to hang on her shoulder.

The darkness made it impossible to find other plants, but she had something to account for her wanderings should any of Craig's men question her. Usually they left her alone. They needed her and her mother. They were the only two people who knew the recipe for the elixir. It had been handed down from her mother's mother, her grandmother. When Everett Howard was their president and his father before him, they left them alone to select the plants and roots needed for the elixir. Craig was an unknown entity and things were changing quickly under his command. It set her on edge more often than not.

Finding the road, she began walking up the edge toward her cabin. Rustling leaves to her right stopped her as she waited to see who was watching. It wasn't an animal, they were quieter than this. Finally, Kent stepped out and stood in the middle of the road.

"What are you doing out here?"

She inhaled and pointed to her sack. "I'm gathering plants for the elixir."

"We're not brewing right now."

"No, we aren't. But I gather all year long. Many of the plants we use have to be dried or propagated and replanted before I use them. You know that, Kent."

He shrugged. "Yeah. I just wanted to see what you said."

Her brows furrowed. "Why?"

"Craig wants us watching everyone right now. He's making some changes and he wants to know what's happening and when."

She nodded. "Okay."

She started walking toward the cabin once again, but Kent stepped in front of her. "Why are you collecting at night?"

"I didn't have time today to get these mushrooms I found. I had to get back and make supper for my mom. I came out here so these wouldn't freeze or wilt."

He stared into her eyes. She stared back. They stood that way for a long time, but she didn't show fear and she didn't look away, even though her heart beat heavily in her chest.

Kent finally stepped aside, though not far enough that

she could walk past without stepping off the road into the brush.

"Watch yourself Elena. I'd suggest not leaving your cabin at night anymore."

"Are we being put on a curfew?"

"Not necessarily a curfew. But it's probably not good for you to be wandering about just the same."

Her lips turned down slightly, but she continued trudging up the hill toward home. It seemed to be a more difficult walk just now. Dread and sadness weighed her shoulders down. What would happen when her mom passed? She'd be at the mercy of this group, and she'd be alone.

She swallowed the large lump that grew in her throat and chided herself on being morose. *Just do what you need to do to survive and maybe what you can do to leave here.*

As she stepped near the edge of the clearing, she saw some activity in the middle. Some of their people gathered around the fire in the evenings to talk or sing. She'd always avoided that because sometimes drama ensued. But now, she might need to join in, at least once in a while, if only for her own protection.

She skirted the first two cabins and neared hers as she heard the singing begin. When they began singing she did enjoy it. There were a few who had beautiful singing voices. Smiling slightly, she opened her cabin door and stepped inside.

The warmth of her little place and the aroma of the soup she'd made earlier lingered in the air. She felt more at home and comfortable than she'd been earlier. It was true what they said: "There's no place like home."

"Is that you, Elena?"

"Yes, Mama."

She set her sack on the table near the washbowl and treaded lightly to her mom's bed. Her mom's sunken eyes stared up at her. The vibrant green they used to be now faded into a milky green. She'd gained weight, though ate very little. She didn't know what was wrong with her mom. Everett had refused to let Elena take her down the hill to a doctor, and even if Craig would now allow it, she had no way to pay for it. The mayor in Glen Hollow refused to let the townspeople trade for elixir and she had nothing else to offer. The medicine woman they had up here, Elenor, had said her mom's heart was weakened. The elixir worked for some heart ailments, but for some reason, didn't work on her mom's.

"Okay. Is everything alright?"

She sat on the edge of the bed and took her mom's right hand in hers. "Everything is fine. I just went out to pick up some mushrooms I'd found earlier today."

"Okay. Craig was looking for you."

"How do you know?"

"He came here."

Fear skittered up her spine and her stomach twisted.

"Did he say what he wanted?"

"No. He just said he wanted to talk to you." Her mom shifted and sat up. Elena fluffed her pillows behind her so she could lean back. "Are you in trouble, Elena?"

"No. I've done nothing wrong, Mama."

Her mom pressed her lips together, but she saw the tremble just before.

She squeezed her mom's hand and looked into her eyes.

"I've done nothing to get us in trouble. Nothing. I promise."

5

Aidyn slid the note into his front pocket and drove to the sewing factory. So someone was watching him. He knew that. Likely the jerk who'd chased him earlier today told Craig and company. He assumed they would. But how did Elena know about it? Were they telling everyone up there to watch for him?

Shaking his head, he turned right and headed toward the factory. He'd worry about it tomorrow. Tonight he planned on getting a good night's sleep after settling into his new room.

As he neared the driveway, he let out a satisfied sigh as he saw his friends' vehicles parked on the property as they unloaded their belongings. He pulled his security card from his pocket and waved it in front of the glass panel. A beep sounded and the gates slowly slid open. It was pretty cool.

Henry waved, then pulled his suitcases from the back of his truck.

Aidyn drove around to the back of the building, where their garage was located, and parked in front of the garage door assigned to him. The third from the left. This was the nicest thing about converting an old factory: the loading docks allowed them plenty of garage space. The ground had been filled in, bringing the doors to ground level, and the doorways had been retrofitted with new doors for each of them, plus two extra for visitors or supplies. At any given time, someone might have a set of parents or siblings coming to visit and they'd be able to park inside as well.

He tapped the garage door opener on his visor. Inside, the garage had been drywalled and painted white. Plenty of lights were installed to keep it bright and his excitement grew at the space provided. He'd scoffed a few weeks ago when Maya told him he'd be excited to live here. They worked a lot and he simply wanted a safe, clean place to sleep and eat. Now he realized what she meant; he was proud that this was his home base and job. The little house they'd been in was nice. This was grand.

He jumped from his truck and pulled his laptop case and suitcase from inside. As he strode through the garage to the back door his eyes darted back and forth, taking in all of the little nuances. Framed posters of car emblems graced the walls: Corvette, Ford, Chevy, and Ram.

"There's more coming." The sound of Sophie's voice turned his head.

Grinning he replied, "Nice."

Her returned smile was genuine. She shrugged, "It was Gaige's idea. But I think it works."

A large delivery truck pulled to a stop near the far end of the garage. A logo on the side read Anderson's Firearm Supply.

His brows furrowed and Sophie laughed. "That is a surprise from your mom and dad. Come see."

He set his suitcase down, laid his laptop case next to it, and followed Sophie across the garage to the end furthest from the living quarters.

Sophie opened a door that led to a small room with two eight-foot tables on either side. There wasn't room for much else. At the end of the table to the right was another door.

She grinned at him before opening the door with a flourish and stepping inside. His parents, Axel and Bridget Dunbar, were hanging heavy rubber mats from a rail that stretched the length of the room. At the far end of the space was a large sectioned-off area with two-foot-high walls.

His mom turned and saw him. She scrambled down her ladder so fast he worried she'd fall. She ran to him and jumped into his arms before he was ready, the impact pushing him back a step or two.

"I missed you, Aidyn."

He wrapped his arms around his mom and held her close. She'd been his rock all his life and he hadn't realized how much he'd missed her too.

"I missed you too, Mom."

Aidyn grinned as his dad neared. "Nice to see you, son. I've missed you, too."

His mom sniffed as he put her down, happy tears swimming in her eyes, and he realized he felt whole now, with them here.

He hugged his dad and whispered back, "I missed you too." After they collected themselves, his mom turned to the room and the work they'd been doing. "Your dad and I felt you all should have a shooting range here. I know you can go out to the base, but this is here. You can blow off steam, practice without foreign eyes watching your every move."

"Wow. That's fantastic. Thank you so much."

His dad grinned. "I've always found shooting a great way to think through some of my issues. Your mom does too, of course, plus she makes money at it. So there's that."

He chuckled. "Yeah, I find shooting a good way to practice while I'm sorting out my thoughts, too. This will be well-used and loved here. Thank you both so much."

His dad nodded. "Go on and settle in. We'll all have dinner together tonight and catch up."

"Thanks, Dad." He hugged his mom briefly and stepped out of the gun range to unpack his suitcase. The excitement that coursed through his body was hard to contain. It seemed to melt the tension of the past few months away in the few minutes he'd been here.

The activity inside was electric as he stepped through the back door. Despite the job of moving, his teammates were laughing, giggling, and excited about all the new things Sophie, Gaige, and his parents had added to their new home. He couldn't wait to share this with them.

6

____

Elena tossed and turned all night. Her nerves felt like tiny pinpricks on her skin. Her body couldn't lie still. Every time she thought about getting up and working on her seeds and plants, she reminded herself she needed to rest. Her head needed to be clear when she spoke to Craig.

Her muscles ached from the tension of the past few months. Mostly since Craig had become president. His changes kept them all on the razor's edge. Uncertainty was the worst form of stress.

Rolling to her left side, she watched her mom sleep for a while. She tried to match her breathing pattern to her mom's, praying it would put her in a state of rest. It didn't. At all.

Rolling to her back, she studied the ceiling in the muted glow of the fire, listened to the crackling of the wood as it burned in the fireplace. She had a good idea what Craig wanted to speak to her about. She'd been dreading it for some time. Everett had spoken to her about it once in the past, but let it drop when she promised to keep brewing the elixir and gathering the roots and plants needed to brew it.

But Craig was a different animal. He had a hard edge. He was angry all the time. He wanted revenge on the townies, and he wouldn't rest until they'd gone to war with them. She didn't relish a life up here with any of these men. They were mostly like Craig. Hard scrabblers who wanted to fight and keep the breach with the townies alive.

The other thing Craig was adamant about was their numbers. He wanted their people to have babies and keep their population from dwindling to nothing. He felt they had a good chance of staving off the townsfolk in any war as long as they had at least a hundred and fifty people. After all, they lived up here. They knew the land. They could hunt and forage and fight and have the advantage should it come to that. But they needed the numbers.

Elena wasn't against marrying or having children. But there was no one up here she wanted to tie herself to forever. Her stomach twisted at the thought of Craig forcing her to marry one of these men. To have to live with their rules. To share a house with one of these fellas who wanted war. Who didn't understand peace. Who felt the townsfolk were taking advantage of them.

And then there was Aidyn. She wanted to know more about him. He wasn't like these men up here. He made her want more. That was likely the biggest danger of them all. *He made her want more.*

But she couldn't leave the mountain. Her mom couldn't make the trek down the mountain, and what would they do to survive?

As far as the outside world was concerned, she was uneducated and poor. She could live off the land, but how long would her mom survive while she tried to build them a shelter and forage for food?

They had a school up here and she knew how to read.

She'd read each book that had found its way up here. She never asked how they got them. She knew of course. But she relished having them. It helped her to read and write and it helped her escape this world and believe in others. She'd read about vampires and werewolves. Those gave her nightmares, but she read those books again and again. She'd read about people's lives. Jackie-O. Johnny Cash. Mark Twain and his friends. She loved them the most.

She felt like a caged animal with no way to break free.

A tear slipped from the corner of her eye and trailed across her cheek before merging with her pillowcase.

A loud crack forced her to bolt upright in her bed. Glancing at her mom, she saw her eyes fly open and seek her out.

Elena put her finger to her lips. Pulling her covers back, she slipped on her heavy wool stockings and her shoes before silently padding to the door. They had two windows in their cabin and both of them had material hanging from the tops to block out the light and nosy people. Moving one of them would no doubt alert someone that she was awake.

The loud crack sounded again, and she jumped and held on to the back of one of their chairs. Putting her ear to their door she listened as voices grew louder. People were leaving their cabins to investigate. But she wasn't about to run into Craig.

Then she heard his voice. "What the hell is going on?"

"He shot at someone coming up the hill," another voice yelled out.

"Did you get him?"

"I don't know."

Her stomach twisted again as she wondered if Aidyn had snuck up the hill. He'd been doing that lately. She'd warned him in her note, but what if he didn't find it?

Tears filled her eyes as she listened for more information.

Craig yelled out. "Go and take a few and find out if you hit him. If you did, bring that fucker back here."

"Kent, Brenner, and Ramsay. Let's go. Bring lanterns."

She turned and pressed her back against the door and focused on her breathing. Closing her eyes she inhaled and let it out slowly. Repeat. Repeat.

"Elena. Do you know who was up here?"

Her eyes flew open as she stared at her mom. She shook her head. "Mama. No. I just don't like all this hatred."

"Elena. You need to tell me what's happening."

"Nothing is happening. Nothing."

7

Aidyn stumbled from his bedroom. The sun hadn't come up yet and the house was mostly dark. He could smell coffee and see the faint glow from lights in the kitchen.

Tate sat on a stool along the back edge of the center island as Lara decorated cookies. Tate was on his phone watching his new wife, but today he wasn't grinning as he watched her.

"What time was that?"

Tate's eyes landed on him and held. "No one from here was up there last night." Tate's brows rose into his hairline as he glanced his way.

Aidyn shook his head as he shuffled to the coffeepot. He'd prefer to have a cup of coffee before heavy conversation if it could be helped.

He nodded at Lara. She smiled in return.

Moving to the coffeepot, he pulled a cup from the shelf above and poured himself some fresh coffee. The aroma rose as he poured and made his mouth water.

There was nothing like the smell of fresh coffee in the morning.

Tate's voice faded into the background as he added some creamer and a half teaspoon of sugar to his black gold and took a tentative sip of the hot brew.

Closing his eyes as the warm liquid slid down his throat he inhaled and turned to face Tate just as he ended his call.

"Morning."

"Morning." Tate laid his phone on the counter. "It appears someone was up the mountain last night and the BRR shot at him or her. I assured the sheriff it was none of us. I'm correct in that, aren't I?"

Aidyn heaved out a breath and took the stool next to Tate.

"You are as far as I'm concerned. I spent the evening chatting with my parents then I dropped into bed around midnight and slept like a baby."

Tate took a drink of his coffee and watched Lara pipe light-blue frosting onto another cookie.

Aidyn absently said, "We did our recon up there yesterday. I don't know who was sneaking up there, but it wasn't us."

"I have a call in to Henry and Maya. They worked last night, and I want to make sure they didn't have to go up there for any reason."

Tate's phone rang as he finished his sentence. "Hey Henry, did anything happen last night?"

Tate listened and Aidyn's thoughts wandered to Elena. Shots went off last night and he sure hoped she wasn't involved in any bullshit up there. He planned on dropping off a basket tonight as soon as it got dark. He worked the night shift for the next three nights. It would be tricky if something had gone on up there. He wondered if there were supplies she needed. He could certainly leave little things in the basket for her.

His eyes landed on the cookies Lara was decorating. He'd leave her a couple of cookies. She probably didn't have the opportunity to eat cookies very often.

Tate ended his call. "Nothing happened last night, but they did hear the shots. They were on the ready, but nothing happened after so they thought the BRR was either trying to coax them away from their post or blowing off steam."

"Either is plausible." He sipped at his coffee.

"What are you doing today?"

"I'm helping Mom and Dad in the shooting range today. We have a few more mats to hang and the bolsters to set up. Then I'll take a nap and get ready for work. What about you?"

"Lara found someone interested in cooking for us. So I'm interviewing her later this morning."

"Sounds fun."

Tate scoffed.

His mom and dad entered the kitchen. "Morning," Bridget said.

"Morning. Did you two sleep good last night?"

His mom kissed his cheek, his dad nudged him as he walked past toward the coffeepot. Bridget sat next to him and sighed. "This kitchen turned out so well."

Lara nodded. "It sure did. I just love it."

"Do you bake these kids fresh cookies every day?"

Lara laughed. "Most days, not all."

Axel set a cup of coffee in front of his wife then leaned against the counter and drank his own.

Soon enough Sophie and Gaige joined them, and the

women started making breakfast. He pulled plates from the cupboards and set the table, then took a walk outside to look around the grounds. From their location here, he could see the mountain Elena lived on. He sat on the picnic table they had outside, his butt on the table, his feet on the seat and stared at the mountain as he waited for his coffee to kick in.

"What's going through your mind?"

He turned at the sound of Spencer's voice. "Nothing. Everything, I guess. I'd like to be a fly in the trees up there to know what Craig Howard is planning. Kent still scares me. His computer skills and world knowledge...and we don't know what supplies or tech they have up there. We know Keaton had a way to call Everett. It's possible Kent had a smartphone for a number of years, and Keaton probably made sure he had the computer gear we found in the shed last year. What we don't know for sure is who else has that same know-how."

Spencer sat beside him on the table and sighed. "I've been thinking that too. They wear rudimentary clothing for the most part. Things that can be made from hides and such, but I've noticed some of them have newer shoes. The last time we were up there, some of the men were wearing modern shirts. Who's supplying them with clothing?"

"Some of it's stolen."

"Some."

His thoughts wandered again as he continued to stare at the mountain. It wasn't unusual for modern ways to seep into other cultures. The BRR could see the towns-people anytime they wanted. What they were wearing and the things they used. If they saw things they liked, they would find a way to obtain or mimic that. He'd like to get a closer look at their everyday life.

8

Elena finished washing up the dishes from the leftover soup they'd eaten this morning. Her wash-bowl sat on the little counter near the window, which had been a table back in the day. Her father cut it in two down the middle and attached both cut sides to the walls of their cabin to give them counter space. He was so proud of how that worked out. The wood was aged now, but she loved how it looked, because her dad was so proud of his work. He'd crafted a shelf underneath for storage.

She turned and wiped the little wooden table in the middle of the room, which served as their dinner table, and she pushed the chairs neatly under. She had to go down to the stream today to bring more water up. It was a trek she made three times a week. Her mom dressed at the back of the cabin near their beds. After, she'd sit in front of the fire for a while working on some sewing or other needlework. She'd taken to helping out some of the others with mending to trade for food or other supplies after Elena took over the brewing. Some of the families shared their meat with them, which they were both grateful for.

Elena knew how to seed potatoes and carrots and she grew rosehips, chamomile, and lemon balm which were used in teas and other cooking. She shared those with the others happily. It wasn't a perfect system, but it worked as well as they needed it to.

Someone knocked on their door and she froze. Her heart raced and dread crawled up her spine. Slowly turning to make sure her mom was dressed, she took a deep breath and padded to the door.

"Yes?"

"It's Craig."

She closed her eyes and swallowed before lifting the board she used as a lock. Just before pulling the door open, she plastered on a smile.

"Good morning."

"Morning. I'd like a minute."

Stepping back to allow him entrance she closed the door behind him, staving off the cold.

"May I get you some tea?"

"No. This won't take long."

She held her hand out toward the table. "Please take a seat."

Her mom shuffled into the room and Elena pulled a chair out for her, nearest the fire.

Craig sat in the chair next to her mom and she sat in the third chair. They only had three chairs. It had been all they needed when her dad was alive.

"I want to thank you for all the years you've helped the Resistance by brewing the elixir. Without it, there are many things up here we wouldn't have." He addressed them both.

Her mom nodded. "Of course."

She chose to remain silent. Her stomach tightened

into a hard knot, and she didn't know if she could form words right now.

"That said, we're in need here. The mayor below has honored our tax deferment for one year. But next year we'll be back to where we were this year. We need money to pay those taxes. The only way to do that is to sell elixir."

Elena whispered. "Okay."

"I'm going to need you to brew a second time this year. Some of the boys have gone off to other towns and found buyers, something Keaton Bennit had promised to do. But we'll need more elixir to do that."

She mentally calculated the supplies she had in store. She'd need more sugar and honey. She would be close with the plants she'd emulsified and stored but she'd have to up production of that.

Swallowing she took a breath. "I think I have enough plant stores. But I'll have to up production of that. I may need help." She glanced at her mom. "Mama can't..."

She cleared her throat to remove the frog that sat firmly inside.

Craig interrupted. "I'll get you help. Elenor's daughter, Theresa, can help you. I understand she's been helping her mom with her medicine. She should be valuable to you."

"Okay." She finally looked Craig in the eyes. "I'll need more sugar."

"I'll have the boys go to Brookswood and get you sugar."

She only nodded. Her breathing finally started to settle and her fingers stopped shaking, though she kept them in her lap just the same.

"Thank you."

"I'll need you to start tomorrow."

She opened her mouth to say something, but it would sound like complaining. Craig held his hand up to stop her. "I'll get the boys to help you with your errands today. I know when you're brewing, things slide. I'll have someone bring up water and I've already sent Brenner and Brock out hunting. They'll get you some meat and smoke it for you. Theresa will be here in a bit to help with household chores."

She swallowed again. "Thank you. That's very kind."

Craig stood and stared down at her. "It's more selfish than kind. We need the money and you need to get brewing. I know this is double the work you usually do so I'm trying to help with that. If you need to forage for plants today, just tell Theresa what is needed here, and she can do your chores. Nothing stands in the way of this second batch. Understand?"

She nodded. "Yes."

Craig left and she exhaled heavily. After a few minutes, she turned to her mom, who sat staring at her.

"Can you do it?"

"I think so. He's offering help, so I should be able to."

"But you were afraid he was here to talk to you about something else."

Elena dropped the lock on the door and tossed another log on the fire.

"Elena?"

"I was afraid he was going to make me marry."

Her mom nodded. "I've been wondering about that. Is there anyone out there you could be interested in?"

"No."

"There will come a day when..."

"No. I don't want to talk about it."

She strode to the back and lifted the lid on her trunk.

She pulled on slacks and heavy socks. Her coat hung by the door. She pulled it on. "Do you have your sewing for today?"

Her mom waved her hand slightly. "I'm fine."

Elena slipped out of the cabin to gulp in some fresh air. She was about to check their storage bin at the back of her cabin when she saw Theresa striding toward her.

"Hi, Elena. Craig said I'm to help you."

She smiled at the sweet girl. She had always been nice to everyone in the camp. At just fourteen she was showing promise in healing with her mom, so Elena could have done worse in the form of help.

"Hi, Theresa. I was going to check my stores and see what else I need for today. If you could help wash the sheets this morning and stack more wood in the bin, I'd appreciate it. Mama is sewing and we've already had breakfast."

"Sure thing. Let me know if there's anything else you need."

9

Dark had fallen a couple of hours ago and the town had begun to settle in for the night. It was nearing ten o'clock and he was on his way to work but wanted to leave a note for Elena.

He laid his note in the bottom of the little basket she'd left for him, set the two cookies from Lara, wrapped in cellophane, on top of the note, then tucked the material over the top and into the sides to keep things from blowing out.

Parking across the road from their ivy-covered spot, he checked the road both ways before exiting his vehicle and making his way across the street. There weren't any street-lights on this section of road, so it helped in concealment.

Pulling the vines up, he tucked the basket into the base of the tree, then laid the vines over it. Jogging across the road to his truck, he felt excitement course through him that he'd left her a note and a treat. It seemed imma-ture to get giddy over something like that, but there was an excitement to their hidden affection or admiration for each other. He'd need to remember to not let the excitement of a forbidden love color his actual feelings. He was too old for that crap. His thirtieth birthday was coming in a couple of months.

He stared at the location of the basket for a few moments before starting his truck. Taking a deep breath, he pulled from his parking spot and headed toward the base and the task at hand tonight.

Upon entering the gates at the base, he parked next to Tate's truck. Tate was walking to the shipping container nearest the road that led up the mountain to Hickory Hills.

Exiting his truck, he jogged to catch up to Tate. "Hey what's up?"

Tate turned and held his forefinger to his lips. Then whispered, "I think someone's messing around over there."

They strode in unison toward the container and heard the tinny sound of something hitting the side of the container.

They ducked and creeped to opposite ends of the container. He ducked down near the south end of the container and pulled his weapon from his ankle holster. Once Tate made it to the other end, he nodded.

Aidyn slid up the side of the container and pushed himself between the two containers butted up to each other. Some of the containers weren't pushed completely to the other and it left a gap. They'd been attaching barriers on the mountain side of the containers to stave off the BRR from slipping between and getting in, but they weren't finished with them.

Peering around the corner to the outside of the container, he saw something move in the brush. Sticking his head out further, he saw Tate watching the same thing he watched. Both of them waited and the movement stopped.

Aidyn glanced up the mountain looking for signs anyone was watching. It was pitch black and the moon was only a sliver. Of course the BRR would use this as an opportunity to plant some of their explosives or cause trouble. They'd need to plan out a bit more, keeping the moon and its cycles in mind.

Tate crept forward toward the movement, his gun pointed at the last spot they'd seen motion. Aidyn covered him from this side and watched for movement from above.

He saw something move a few feet above Tate's head and whistled.

Tate looked up to where Aidyn pointed and aimed his gun up just in case.

Aidyn took deep breaths to control his breathing, the adrenaline was making it difficult at the moment.

All movement stopped and they waited for a few minutes before deciding it was an animal. Tate scooted back to the gap between the containers on his end, but Aidyn watched for a while longer.

He stepped back between the two containers when the movement started again. He froze and peered around once more seeing the hind end of a man running across the road and diving into the large brush and trees on the other side.

He stepped back and motioned to Tate, who jogged to him.

"There was someone out there. I just saw his ass run across the road and disappear into the woods."

"Shit. I'll go grab the sensor and see if it detects explosives. Don't go close until we check it."

"Roger."

His heartbeat increased and he felt sweat gather at the middle of his back even though it was only forty-two degrees tonight. He swallowed to wet his throat and inhaled deep breaths to calm himself. He'd made it through two tours in Afghanistan without getting blown up. He'd like that streak to continue.

Tate's footsteps crunched on the gravel behind him. "Okay, let's see what we can find."

He flipped the switch on their explosive detector and the lights flashed as it came to life. Finally all turning green, Tate laid it on the ground and pushed it lightly toward the area they'd first saw movement. The little wheels on the detector bumped over the uneven terrain but one of the lights began blinking red.

"Shit."

"Yeah."

Aidyn blew out a breath. "I've never dismantled an explosive."

Tate shook his head, "Me either."

"We may need to ask Myles to come down while these assholes are using explosives."

"I think you're right about that."

Aidyn huffed out a breath. "I'll go grab those bolsters we have in the end container. We'll toss those on top of the explosive for tonight and if it blows, we'll have deadened it somewhat."

"Good idea."

Aidyn strode to the end container and pulled it open. Grabbing the end of one of the bolsters, he heaved it up over his shoulder and began dragging it to Tate's location. His heart rate increased from the exertion, these bolsters weighed about a hundred pounds each and were eight feet long. They were a bitch to move around.

Together he and Tate muscled one to the edge of the grounds then each of them grabbed an end and swung it hammock style and let it fly to land over the explosive. As soon as they'd released their end, they both ran for cover as the explosion sounded and the earth shook.

10

———

A blast shook the entire mountain. At least that's what it felt like. Elena sat bolt upright in bed and listened as voices grew outside.

"Mama, stay inside. I'll go see what happened."

"Elena, maybe you should stay in here."

She tossed her covers back and stood. "I won't be long. Stay here."

Scrambling to pull her socks on and dress quickly, her brain started working again and dread filled her belly.

She grabbed her jacket from the hook and slipped her arms into the sleeves. She threw another log on the fire, then slipped outside.

Theresa ran toward her, her eyes round in fear.

"Are you and Grace alright?"

"Yes. Just a bit scared. What happened?"

"I heard some guys talking and they said there was an explosion down at the base."

Elena's hands flew to her face. "Oh no." Her heart fluttered and her stomach tightened.

Theresa nodded. "They can't find Ramsay."

Craig entered the center of their community and started barking out orders.

"Brenner, go find Ramsay. I told you little shits to stop using explosives down there."

Craig turned and ordered everyone else to their cabins. "Go to bed. Everyone." Then his eyes landed on her. "Elena, you have a busy day tomorrow. Get some rest."

She patted Theresa on the shoulder. "Go on so you don't get in trouble. I'll see you tomorrow."

Theresa moved toward her cabin off to the right of Elena's. Elena turned and silently entered the cabin, dropping the lock in place.

After she hung her coat on the hook, she turned to see her mom sitting up in bed, waiting for news.

"It seems some of the boys were using explosives down by the base. They're looking for Ramsay."

"Oh dear. All this antagonism is going to start a war. We barely slipped away from one last fall. The townspeople aren't going to tolerate all of this nonsense for long."

"I know, Mama."

Elena poured some water into the pot over the fire. She dropped rosehips inside to steep then pulled a chair away from the table and sat down. She fought the urge to go and see what happened. What if Aidyn had been hurt? She knew he was a target. Most of the folks up here blamed him for Everett's death. And Craig liked to use it as a way to incite violence when it was convenient. Secretly, Craig had coveted his father's position for a long time and made no bones about wanting things to change. He thought his father had gone too soft and let the new mayor cut them out of earnings they could make with the purpose of eventually disbanding them and making them live by townie rules and laws. Craig had no intention of following their laws. Ever.

The water came to a boil and Elena pulled her cup from the counter. Glancing at her mom, who still sat upright in bed, she shook her head. "I can't sleep now. See if you can, Mama."

Her mom scooted down and laid her head on her pillow once more and Elena poured some tea into her cup and sat once again. She'd give them about an hour or so to settle down outside, then she was going to sneak down and check the basket for a note from Aidyn, and then see if things were alright at the base. She'd be busy tomorrow beginning a new batch of elixir so she'd be busy for the next few days.

Voices grew louder outside and she went to the window and lifted a corner of the fabric slightly to see if she could see anything. She saw Brenner and Ramsay walk into the center court. Craig hit Ramsey in the face, causing him to fall back into Brenner.

Ramsay put his hands up to stave off anything more, but Craig got into his face and sternly said something, though she couldn't hear what. Craig stalked off toward his cabin and Brenner and Ramsay skulked off to theirs.

She briefly wondered why Kent wasn't involved, but she had seen him and Craig talking a couple of times recently and suspected Craig had Kent working on some secret project that was no doubt going to cause trouble below.

Dropping the fabric, she sat heavily and stared into the fire. All this hate and violence made her stomach twist. What would finally be the end of it all?

As she finished her second cup of tea, she quietly

pulled her jacket from its hook, pulled on the old, ripped gloves she wore, and grabbed her sack from beside the fireplace before silently slipping out of the cabin.

She quickly stepped around the side of her cabin, then slipped down the mountain from behind. Moving slowly until her eyes further adjusted to the darkness, she followed her usual path, so noise was minimal. As soon as she dropped down far enough to be seen from above, she adjusted her direction slightly toward her basket. Her senses were keen as she moved stealthily through the familiar woods. She'd been slipping out for years. This was her favorite time to explore the mountain. It had started when she began foraging, but over the years, she found a love of the quiet. No hatred. No disruption as the earth slept for a couple of hours before the sun appeared in the sky and changed the landscape from dark to light.

Easily creeping through the trees, she found her tree, the one where her basket hopefully had been replaced. The air in her lungs seized until they burned and she dragged in a breath. What if he didn't respond? Of course, he didn't owe her anything. But she found such happiness in conversing with him. Squaring her shoulders, she inched forward and lifted the vines. Her heart pranced in her chest when she saw her basket. He'd brought it back!

Her body shook with anticipation as she neared it. Lifting the handle, she felt some weight in it and her excitement grew again.

She scrambled to her path, then changed her course and found the little patch of mandrake she'd been growing and nurturing. Snapping some of the leaves and putting them into her basket, she added a few more fresh plants she'd use in her brew today. If she was questioned, she'd say she couldn't sleep and wanted to get ahead of the brewing for the day.

She continued up the mountain, finally arriving at her cabin. Slipping inside, she set her basket on the counter and took her jacket off. The first rays of the sun peered over the mountain, but her excitement wouldn't let her wait any longer. She filled her cup once again with tea, checked that her mom was still sleeping then brought her little basket to the table. She scooped the plants off the top, then lifted the material to see two cookies like the ones she'd seen in Lara's bakery the couple of times she'd looked inside. She stared at them for a long time. They were the most beautiful things she'd ever seen. Light-blue frosting topped with white frosted swirls graced the cookie. It looked like fancy lace. Like she'd seen in books.

She opened the cellophane as quietly as she could and bit the very end of the cookie. It was sweet and a cross between chewy and crispy. It was delectable and the best thing she'd ever eaten in her life. The closest thing she had up here for a sweet treat was when they had some leftover sugar from brewing and they browned it, then put it in a pan and let it cool. Their own homemade suckers. Sometimes they'd flavor it with herbs for something different.

She took another bite of her cookie and closed her eyes as she ate it.

Her mom rolled over and Elena froze and waited for her to settle again. She looked in the basket again and saw Aidyn's note at the bottom.

Her fingers shook as she lifted the bright white paper from the bottom of the basket. He'd folded it over once and she opened it, thrilled when she saw his writing.

"Thank you for the note. I hope things are going okay for

you up there. I've heard shooting and I hope you're safe. I swiped a couple of Lara's cookies for you. She makes a good cookie. If there is anything else you need or prefer, please let me know. I'm happy to get things for you to help make your life easier. I enjoy reading your notes and hope we can talk in person soon. — A"

11

Aidyn rolled to his back and looked over where Tate had been standing. "Tate." He croaked then coughed.

"Over here."

He turned to his right and saw Tate trying to stand from where he lay on the ground.

Letting out a breath, Aidyn rolled and got to his feet. He stumbled as his body righted itself. His ears rang and the dust floating in the air made visibility difficult.

Tate met him halfway between where they each landed, and they stood silently for a few minutes as they surveyed the damage.

The container directly in front of the explosion took the brunt of the damage. It sat at a tilted angle, the back side of it clearly misshapen.

Tate finally asked, "Are you alright?"

He coughed again, then cleared his throat. "Yeah." He shook his head and dust flew around him. He was instantly sorry he did that as the coughing started again.

"It's just the dust. I'm going to the trailer for a bottle of water."

Tate stumbled along with him. The ringing in his ears began to subside and his heartbeat slowed to almost normal.

The trailer felt like a welcoming home at this point. The light inside helped him to see. He turned to Tate and laughed. "You should see yourself."

Tate stared at him a moment. "You should see yourself. You look like a giant dust mite."

He shuffled to the small mirror on the wall above the file cabinet and laughed. There wasn't a place on him not covered in dust. It was thick on his eyebrows; his hair, even though he'd shaken it outside, still had a coat of dust on it. He looked like an old decoration shoved in the back of an old basement. The only bright thing on his face were his eyes and even they were dirty and bloodshot.

He pulled two bottles of water from the fridge. Handing one to Tate, he cracked his open and slugged down most of it. The cold liquid felt good sliding down his throat. The refreshing ice water sluicing the dust from his throat renewed him.

He took a couple of breaths, then finished the water before grabbing another one from the fridge and tucking it in his back pocket.

He headed back to the door, careful not to leave a terrible dust trail behind him. As he stepped outside, he felt like he could take a deeper breath without coughing. Headlights showed near the gate and he called in to his partner. "Someone's coming."

Tate and Aidyn clomped down the metal steps and awaited the approaching vehicle, which turned out to contain Spencer and Henry.

"We heard the explosion and looked at the cameras. Are you two alright?" Spencer called out.

He nodded. "Yeah. We just went in for water and were about to assess the damage now that the dust is settling."

A police squad drove into the lot and the four of them stood and waited for whoever was in it to stop.

A female cop exited the vehicle and walked toward them.

"Hello. I'm Officer Maria Bradley. Are you alright?"

Tate stepped forward first. "Yes ma'am. I'm Tate Vickers. This is my team, Aidyn Dunbar, Spencer Lawson, and Henry Delany."

Officer Bradley nodded in greeting then looked around the area. "What happened?"

Tate pointed toward the container. "We were just about to assess the damage. Aidyn and I saw one of the BRR plant an explosive. We had enough time to toss a bolster on it, which deadened the blast a fair amount. But we haven't gotten a good look at anything yet."

He and Henry and Spencer worked their way toward the container, watching the ground closely for any debris. He pulled the flashlight off his belt and lit the way, mostly shining on the container. Upon closer inspection, it had been moved about eight inches from its original spot and didn't look safe anymore. He shone his flashlight on the space between the container and its neighboring container then turned to Spencer and Henry.

"We took the bolster from that container and had just enough time to toss it on when the explosion happened."

Henry looked at the area where the explosion had taken place by shining his flashlight on it. "You likely set the explosion off with the bolster, but it sure would have been a lot worse if you hadn't tossed it on."

"We didn't know if they had it on a timer or if something else would trigger it."

"Good call."

Spencer began carefully inspecting the end of the container, in case there was more. Henry inspected the opposite end, and he followed the path the BRR kid followed up the hill. He checked his phone and saw it had been a little more than an hour since the blast. He and Tate must have been knocked out for a bit. That would explain his headache.

He shone his light on the path of trampled weeds and brush the kid followed, looking for any traces of more explosives, timers, or wires. The cool crisp air felt good, the tall brush helped to dust him off.

He saw the footprints across the road and scooted across and into the woods. There was blood on the ground, and he followed that trail for a few feet. A bloody piece of metal lay in the path and he picked it up. It was sharp and looked as though it had imbedded itself in the kid who ran from the explosion. He kind of deserved it, the little fucker.

He shined his light around the area and wondered if Elena had gotten the basket. He didn't have time to search there. The others would be waiting for him, but he bet she'd heard the explosion. Likely the entire town and mountain did.

Heaving out a big breath, Aidyn turned toward the base, looking for anything else that he could bring down.

His teammates and Officer Bradley were on this side of the container, their lights shining on it and the damage when he neared.

Spencer turned, "Did you find anything?"

"I found a bloody piece of shrapnel and a blood trail.

He got hit with some of whatever he filled the bomb with."

Henry pointed his light at the side of the container. "Metal. A lot of it. Good thing this was between you and Tate."

Pieces of metal had speared the side of the container. Some of the holes were bigger than his head, where the bulk of the shrapnel had hit. The heavy rubber bolster lay in a heap close to where they'd tossed it. A chill ran down his spine.

12

Elena spent the morning boiling the plants she needed in heavy pots over the fire. Her brewing station was under a large pavilion-like structure to keep rain out of the brew, covered, yet open so workers helping her could carry wood and sugar in to her without dealing with doors. Also, this early part of the brew was the most dangerous. Toxic chemicals filled the air. She wore heavy coverings over her nose and mouth to keep from inhaling the fumes. Anyone approaching during this stage did the same.

She labored at a workbench built along one side of the semi-structure. Her plants and herbs were separated out and she currently used a large knife to cut mandrake and other plants into smaller pieces, so they used every inch of the plants. No one was to touch the plants except her. Mostly because some of them were actually deadly if ingested in raw form. Somehow, they always procured rubber gloves for her to wear while working in the earliest stages of the brew.

The bubbling behind her grew in intensity and she

knew it was time to drop the mandrake into the water. She waited as Cole Honeycutt and Brayden Lowe stacked the wood they'd brought into the area. She didn't like their presence while she brewed. They were both on Craig's council and she felt judged by them. There was no particular reason why. Lately, she felt that way about anyone associated with Craig. They all wanted war with the citizens below and they exuded hate and anger.

After they walked away, she hung her yellow flag on the outside of the structure, letting everyone know this was not the time to come near. It was her favorite time. Prying eyes would stay away and she could work in peace.

She saw everyone outside turn and enter their cabins and she was glad she wore a face covering because they couldn't see her smile.

She scraped her mandrake and herbs together into an old metal pot, one she'd used for years now and her mom before her. Then she shook the pot over the boiling water and let them fall inside. Repeating this for the other two boiling pots, she worked slowly and methodically. It was work she'd done for years and she was good at it. She loved being alone. No one to direct. No one to ask questions of her. No one to feel as though she were performing. Though, she had no doubt, they were watching from their windows.

After dropping in the herbs one by one, she stirred each pot and added water as needed. This would continue for a few hours, boiling the juices and extracts from the plants. She'd add more throughout the day and tomorrow, these pots would be strained of the bits and pieces that didn't boil down and she'd begin the slow process of adding the sugar.

After she stopped for the evening, the pots would be

covered, and the water inside would rest. It was during that time she'd retire to her cabin, eat something, and sneak down to leave her basket for Aidyn.

Her tummy flipped when she thought about him. He'd given her cookies. Beautiful cookies. Other than her parents and one man up here who tried to woo her years ago, she didn't get gifts. Certainly not something as delicious as those cookies were. She sadly broke them into small pieces so she could take a little bite throughout the day. She carried them in her apron right now. Close to her body and safe from anyone else seeing them. Aidyn's note was tucked into her shoe. She should have burned it in the fireplace last night, but she couldn't bring herself to do it. He had great handwriting. It was neat and though she struggled with a couple of the words, she could read it.

She moved calmly to the next pot and stirred, lost in thought. It was her purpose for being up here and earning her keep. She knew nothing else and that made her sad. She was stuck here. At least for as long as her mom was alive. After that, she'd see. Maybe she could cook for another town. She'd have to get there. Maybe Aidyn would be willing to help her. She nurtured that thought for a while because it kept her mind occupied while she stirred. Moving to the third pot, she repeated her stirring.

Once all pots were stirred, she added wood to each fire and jumped when she noticed Theresa at the edge of the shelter.

"I didn't mean to scare you. I brought you lunch. You've been out here a long time."

Theresa laid a plate, covered with a towel, on the end of the workbench.

"Thank you, Theresa. I appreciate it."

"Of course. Thank you for brewing and helping us all out. We appreciate you and your dedication to us."

Ouch. Guilt filled her body and her heartbeat increased painfully. She wasn't dedicated. She felt like a trapped animal, unable to leave here and unable to survive anywhere else.

She nodded at Theresa. "Of course. This is my home."

Theresa nodded, apparently happy with her response, then turned and ambled back to her cabin.

Elena slipped her gloves off and laid them away from her food, then lifted the towel and found smoked venison and fresh biscuits. She ate her food slowly, enjoying the flavor. She'd never mastered biscuits for some reason. Her mom had tried many times to teach her and so did the other women up here, but it wasn't something that came naturally to her.

Lara could probably make the best biscuits, if her cookies were anything to gauge from. Then she wondered if Aidyn liked biscuits and figured he did. Didn't everyone? She couldn't make him fresh biscuits either, in exchange for the cookies. But she could make him a bracelet. She had some tanned leather in her trunk. It was from her father when he was alive. He was so good at tanning hides, and she kept scraps from his many projects. He'd made her the leather apron she wore with all the pockets in it. He told her she could put plants and herbs in the pockets when she foraged. She rarely wore it when she foraged though. She wanted to keep it clean and safe from damage.

"What are you lost in thought about?"

Her head jerked up to see Craig watching her from across the brewing area and her stomach knotted.

13

He'd slept most of the day. After the night he'd had he'd dropped off into a deep sleep and didn't hear a single noise in the house. Though, it could be the house. The old factory was well built and had been insulated during the remodel for energy efficiency and quiet.

He stood from his bed and looked across the new wood floors to the trail of dust he'd left after getting home this morning. It led from his doorway to his bathroom.

He stumbled to the bathroom and pulled his used towel off the hook where he hung it to dry, then wiped up his mess. They still didn't have a housekeeper, so they were on their own. Even so, he'd been taught better than to live like a pig, so he cleaned.

He dressed and entered the kitchen to a lively discussion from his teammates about what they wanted to call the house. They'd all been calling it the sewing factory, but it wasn't that anymore.

Maya turned as he entered the room. "Here, Aidyn, you need to write a few names on pieces of paper and we're going to look at them all and decide."

"Can I have coffee first?"

Adelaide laughed. "If you make it. It's two in the afternoon. The coffee stopped brewing hours ago."

He glanced at the clock on the wall and frowned. "Okay, I'll get a cola instead."

His teammates were quiet as they wrote their suggestions on pieces of paper, he wasn't awake enough yet to partake in this bit of creative energy.

He sat on a stool at the counter and watched Adelaide scribble away. She had a list. The last name on the list was, "Hemmed In."

Aidyn chuckled. "You're all getting too creative for me."

He stood and opened the refrigerator. He found some leftover ham his mom and Sophie had made yesterday and pulled it out. Carrying it to the other counter, he pulled a plate from the cupboard and stabbed three slices with a fork and dropped them on his plate.

Tate sauntered into the kitchen with a grin on his face. "I found someone to cook and clean for us. She starts tomorrow. Her name is Helissa. She's in her fifties, not that it matters, and she's a widow. She's looking for a job and feels this will give her plenty to do. She's off on the weekends but will have meals in the fridge for us. And Lara has known her for a few years and says she's reliable and even-tempered. Let's keep her that way."

Aidyn chuckled. "That's fantastic. I was just wondering what we'd do when the ham was gone."

Addy shook her head and wrote down another name idea on her sheet of paper. Tate grabbed a bottle of water from the fridge. "Also, Myles will be joining us in a couple of weeks. It appears we need someone here who understands explosives better than most folks."

Maya grinned. "He won't say it, but he's excited about getting here. Since Tate and Lara got married, he thinks we're all having the time of our lives here."

Tate shook his head. "Why would he think that? We're looking for an explosive's expert."

She nodded. "I know and I told him it isn't all fun and games here, but he said you managed rather well for yourself."

Tate laughed. "If he's looking for a wife, Lara can likely find someone for him. Shianne is available."

Maya held her hands up as if staving off a slap. "Oh, no, no, no. That girl talks too much. She'll drive me crazy."

Aidyn chuckled. "I thought we were talking about Myles."

Maya glared at him from across the counter. "Anyone Myles marries will be my sister-in-law. It matters a lot."

Aidyn laughed as he sat at the counter once again and ate his ham.

Tate strode to his end of the counter. "You okay Aid?"

"Yeah. Are you?"

"Yeah. Just checking. PTSD and all."

He sat straighter and looked Tate in the eye. "I'm okay, Bud. I'll admit to being rattled last night, but I'm good now. Any word on the explosives?"

"Spencer and Henry are there with an explosives team from Brookswood. I'm on my way there now."

He stood. "I'll go with you. I'll take my truck though. I've got some errands to run afterwards."

He wanted to see what they were up against. And he wanted to see if Elena had replaced the basket. As he strode passed Tate he said, "I'll meet you out there. I'm grabbing my hoodie and gloves."

"Roger."

In his room he grabbed the notebook he'd purchased to write Elena notes and a pen. He'd find some time to write to her if she replaced the basket, and if she needed anything, he'd run to the store after he saw the explosives and heard what the experts thought about it.

As he drove to the construction site, he watched the mountain to see if he could catch sight of her. She moved like a ghost so he doubted she'd let herself be seen, but he hadn't seen her in person in several weeks now. They'd been conversing strictly by basket and notes.

That likely wouldn't change anytime soon. He was a wanted man up there and she wasn't allowed to come down the mountain per Craig's new mandate.

He parked next to Tate's truck and strode across the dirt toward the far side where the explosion happened last night. There were four men with Tate, and they were looking at something at the base of the container.

Tate glanced at him as he neared. "This is Aidyn Dunbar, my teammate and the man who was with me last night. Aidyn, this is Dylan from Tech Labs in Brookswood."

Aidyn shook Dylan's hand. "Nice to meet you."

"Please tell Aidyn what you just told me," Tate said.

He swallowed as he listened to Dylan explain what they'd figured from last night, then turned to look at the explosives, or what was left of them on the ground.

"What did they use?"

"It was a regular pipe bomb. We found pieces of it and matched it up to the pipe being used here on the construction site to run the wires through."

"Fucking pieces of shit not only stole the pipe but then tried to blow us up with it."

Tate pointed to a pile of screws, nuts, and bolts lying

on the ground near the edge of the container. "They also stole the shrapnel they used in it."

Aidyn shook his head and huffed out a breath. "We don't know how many more of these they have planned."

Dylan neared the explosion site. "The bolster you threw on top forced most of the blast into the ground. It would have been catastrophic had you not tossed it on. The debris would have gone about eleven hundred feet. I suspect this was a five-pound bomb or so."

"How was it detonated?"

Dylan scratched the side of his face but continued looking at the hole in the ground. It was at least five feet deep and at least six feet wide.

"I did find a lead wire." He pointed to the wire, now laying on top of the brush. "But I think the bolster had a lot to do with detonation. That's not necessarily a bad thing. If they were waiting for people to be around, this would easily have killed someone."

Aidyn shook his head and tried to slow his breathing. Anger rushed through his body, and he felt the sweat drip down his back. He turned to Tate. "We're all going to need to wear Kevlar until we know there won't be more of this."

Tate nodded. "Dylan and his crew are doing a sweep today, so we'll know for today we're good. I'm taking Henry or Spencer up to speak with Craig."

"I'll go with you."

Tate shook his head. "I don't think that will do anything but anger him right now. You need to stay down here."

He heaved out a breath. "Yeah." He turned to go but turned back to Tate. "You need me for anything right now?"

"No. Get some rest, we're on tonight."

He nodded. "Thank you, Dylan."

Dylan nodded. "You're welcome."

He stomped to his truck and huffed out a big breath once inside. He took a long drink from his water bottle then drove out of the construction site and toward the parking lot across from the tree where they'd exchanged the basket.

Settling in, he watched the road and the activity in this section of town and found it rather empty. He swallowed before jumping from his truck and striding across the road. He crossed the road and stepped into the vines at the edge of the road and lifted them. No basket. He looked around it a bit in case she set it somewhere else. Nothing.

He tried not letting the disappointment wash over him. So far today was a sucky day. *What do you do on a sucky day? Go back to bed, that's what.*

14

Elena swallowed as she reminded herself Craig was cagey. He probably meant to set her nerves on edge.

Grateful she had a covering on her face, she replied. "I just love this part of the brewing process is all. I allow myself the privilege to immerse myself in it."

It was total bullshit. And he must not have liked the answer all that much because he turned and stalked away. She set out to stirring her pots again and adding water where needed until it was time to let the water rest.

As dusk neared, she stretched her shoulders and her back and set the lids on the pots for the night. Using a long metal rod, she dispersed the wood under the kettles so only a few embers remained, though the heat would last for a few hours. By morning when she came out here, they'd likely still be warm, though only to the touch. Of course it was cooler right now than when she normally brewed, so it could be a bit different. But it wouldn't change anything with the brew.

After she finished with her chores, she pulled her gloves off, cleaned up the workbench she used and collected her knives to wash. Striding across the brewing grounds toward home she glanced around to see if people were milling about. Most of them would stay inside tonight because of her brewing. Tomorrow would be another day as they'd all feel like the danger was over and they'd be watching her.

Entering her cabin, her mom sat at the table with a plate of food in front of her. "Hi, Mama. How are you feeling?"

"Better. I got quite a bit of mending done today. Theresa made you a supper plate. It's on the counter."

Elena hung up her jacket and washed her hands in the wash basin. Taking her plate to the table, she lifted the towel laying over it and inhaled the fresh aroma of baked beans and smoked venison.

"It smells good. She's a good cook for such a young one."

"I bet she's been cooking for years already. Her ma is always working."

"You're probably right, Mama."

She ate a few bites of her venison and savored the flavor of the beans.

"How did your brew go today?"

She swallowed her beans. "Good. It's always peaceful the first day."

"It is. Hard work, though."

"Yeah. I can feel it in my back today."

Her mom said nothing so she continued to eat. "I saw Craig watching you today."

At the mention of his name her tummy twisted. "Yeah." She scooped another spoonful of beans up. "Why do you think he did that?"

Her mom pulled her venison apart with her fingers. "I don't know. I also don't like it."

She ate her spoonful of beans. "I don't either."

Her mom finished supper and took her plate to the wash basin and washed it. Elena finished her meal but before she stood to wash her plate her mom took it from the table and washed it for her.

"You've had a hard day. I've got this."

"Thanks, Mama."

"Did you see those men from town come up here today?"

She froze and struggled to swallow the last bite of supper. "What men?"

She didn't see Aidyn. He wouldn't come up here, would he?

"That one that Lara married. Tate. And the other one, the big one. I don't know his name."

"I didn't see them. Did you?"

"No. Theresa told me they came up to see Craig."

She wondered if that was before or after he'd watched her brew. Her imagination ran wild; that was guilt. Craig had no idea she and Aidyn were writing notes to each other. "Do you know what they wanted?"

"Theresa said something about the explosion last night."

She let out a breath, nice and slow, and stared into the fire. That made perfect sense. Of course, they'd come up and talk to Craig about that.

Her mom rubbed her shoulders from behind and the goosebumps skittered down her spine. "Oh, Mama, that feels so good."

"I know. Your daddy used to do this for me when I brewed."

Elena took some deep breaths and allowed herself to relax. "Thanks, Mama."

"You're welcome." She wiped the counter down. "Are you going to wash up tonight? I'm about ready for bed."

"Yes. I'll make it quick."

She poured water into their big kettle and slid it in the fireplace to warm. She pulled fresh clothing from her trunk and laid them on her bed. They washed up back here in the winter. In the summer months they'd go down to the creek and bathe.

She pulled a towel from the holder on the wall, grabbed a bar of the handmade lavender soap from the dish it laid on, and placed them on her bed. She pulled the hot kettle from the fireplace and carried it to the back. She collected two basins from under the counter; one to wet and soap her cloth in and the other, clean water to rinse with.

Closing the curtain, she undressed and bathed.

She heard her mom sit in a chair in front of the fire and wondered what it was like bathing in town. They had bathrooms down there. At least that's what she'd heard, and a thing called a shower. Kent told them all that a shower sprayed water over your body, and you could make it as warm or cool as you wanted. That must be wonderful.

Dressing in her clean clothes, she stuffed her dirty ones in the old pillowcase they used as a laundry bag. She'd ask Theresa to help with the laundry this week. Pushing open the curtain, she carried her dirty water out and set it on the counter. Hanging the kettle back on the hook near the fire, she pulled her coat on, then put her leather apron over the top of it.

"I'll be back in a bit, Mama. I'm dumping this water

and taking a little time for myself. I'll see you in the morning."

"Don't get into trouble, Elena."

"I won't."

She stepped from the cabin, grateful no one was around, and that dark had settled over the mountain. Ducking quickly behind her cabin, she poured the dirty water onto the ground and set the basin on the stack of wood. She picked up her basket with the material in it and found her path down to the base of the mountain.

She listened for sounds and took in large breaths as she enjoyed the peacefulness. Lifting a piece of the cookie from her apron, she nibbled on it, savoring the sweetness in her mouth. She heard a truck at the foot of the mountain and ducked down into the brush near the edge of the woods. Another truck followed it, and she followed the sounds as they parked at the construction site of the base.

She inched closer to the base, careful not to be seen and watched Aidyn and Lara's man, Tate, leave their trucks and walk into the trailer. Her heart skipped a beat then fluttered rapidly in her chest. She found it hard to take in a deep breath and her stomach twisted.

The door to the trailer opened again; the men stepped out and looked around. They split up and Aidyn walked toward the edge of the site near the mountain. She scooted closer. Silently. She navigated the downed branches as if she knew where each of them lay. Near the bottom of the mountain, she scooted across the road near the base and froze.

15

Aidyn's eyes rounded. "Are you watching me?"

Elena nodded. She looked beautiful. The faint light from the perimeter lights at the construction site illuminated her green eyes. He found it difficult to look away from her.

"You aren't taking information back to Craig are you?"

Her brows bunched together, and he saw the surprise on her face. "No." She whispered.

"Can you talk?"

She turned her head and looked up the mountain. He reached out and touched her hand, her skin was cool and she didn't have gloves on. His breath caught when she turned her hand and took hold of his. Shivers ran up his arm. His stomach flipped.

"I have a place we can talk."

She allowed him to pull her into the brush and to the construction site. The only place he could think of for them to talk was inside one of the containers. He lifted the metal handle on the end container and rotated it. He pulled the door open, then stepped inside, gently pulling her along with him. He pulled the door to, leaving it open a sliver so the lights would shine in. He wanted to look at her.

He kept his voice soft when he spoke. "Are you alright? I worried the explosion last night affected you."

"I'm fine. I heard it. It shook the cabin. But I was mostly worried about you."

Her voice was like listening to his favorite song. She had a soft, sweet, voice.

He reached out and ran the backs of his fingers down her cheek. Her skin was like satin. Her eyes locked on his. "I've wanted to touch you for so long."

He saw her throat move as she swallowed. He stepped closer to her, and her right hand reached up to touch his face. Then floated into his short beard.

"It's soft. I wasn't sure if it would be."

He took a deep breath and let it out. He shook as he exhaled. He touched hair. The dark silky strands felt good on his fingers. He slowly dipped his head down, allowing her time to pull away. When she didn't, his heart raced in his chest. When his lips touched hers, his body shook.

Her hands slid around his waist and hugged him. His tongue licked along her lips. She let his tongue slide in. She tasted like...cookies. He remained gentle with her. Fitting his lips to hers. Tentatively sweeping his tongue into her mouth, enjoying the feel of her tongue in his mouth. Her body pressed close to his felt like heaven.

Goosebumps rose on his skin as they explored each other. She smelled like lavender. He pulled away and stared into her eyes. "I've thought about doing that since I first saw you."

She smiled and it made him gape in amazement. She was stunning. "I thought about kissing you too."

The sound of a door slamming outside brought him around to the present and their circumstance. "Tate will be wondering where I am."

"I can't be gone long either. Craig is watching me closely right now."

"Why?"

"I'm not sure exactly. He's making me start a second brew to make money for the taxes. I started it today. He watched me a lot today, which was weird."

"Are you in danger?" His heart broke for her. He couldn't protect her up there.

"I don't think so."

"Please let me know if you ever feel in danger."

"Aidyn, you can't come up there."

"I will to protect you. In a minute."

He kissed her again. This time it felt rushed.

He pulled away and stared at her. She pulled a sheet of paper from her apron and handed it to him. "I was going to leave this for you. Thank you for the cookies. They were delicious."

"I could taste them on you when I kissed you."

She pulled a pocket open on her apron. "I had to break them apart and put them in here so no one would find them. I nibble on them when I think I'm not being watched."

His heart sank. She lived like a caged animal, and it was disheartening. "I'm sorry Elena. I'm so sorry."

She smiled, her eyes locked on his. "Please don't do anything to get yourself in trouble. I'll try to come down tomorrow and see you."

"Okay."

He kissed her quickly, then turned and peered out the door. He didn't see Tate anywhere, so he reached back and took her hand in his and pulled her from the container. He quickly ran with her to the edge of the road.

She squeezed his hand, then disappeared into the woods across the road. He couldn't even hear her move.

Deflated, he swallowed the lump in his throat, then closed the container and pushed the lock closed. He glanced toward the woods once more, then strode across the construction site to the trailer. He evened his breathing as he walked and squeezed his stomach muscles and let them out to quell the roiling inside. He'd find a way to help her. There had to be a way.

Clomping up the metal steps to the trailer office, he pocketed Elena's note, then took another breath before entering.

"There you are. Everything okay out there?"

"Yeah." He pulled a bottle of water from the refrigerator. "I'll go out again in an hour and do another check."

"Okay."

He sat heavily in a chair and watched Tate log on to the cameras. He'd need to remember that they could be seen on security footage. Maybe he'd find another place for them to meet.

Tate clicked through the cameras and watched the area for movement. Aidyn wanted to read Elena's note, so he stood and went into the bathroom.

Quietly opening the paper, he read her note.

"Please be careful down there. Craig was pissed at Ramsay for the explosion last night but that doesn't mean they won't try again. Thank you for the cookies, they were delicious. I've never had a cookie, but I've looked in Lara's bakery window and saw them. So sweet. Anything I bring up here needs to be hidden, so

I can't think of anything at the moment. Is there anything I can get for you? - E"

He folded her note and tucked it in his pocket. Flushed the toilet, then washed his hands. Or pretended to. He could still smell her hair on them and he didn't want to wash that away.

16

Elena slipped up the mountain and picked up her wash basin. Rounding the side of her cabin, she stepped to the door and entered quietly.

A quick glance to the back, she saw her mom breathing steadily, a slight snore coming from her. She should be exhausted but instead she was wired. She crept to the trunk she kept at the foot of her bed and silently lifted the lid. She pulled the spool of tanned hide rope from the corner and closed the lid.

Quietly moving a chair to the fire so she could see, she unspooled some of the leather and cut strips. Using a four-strand braiding method, she began braiding the leather strips together. At the halfway point, she added a pretty cat-eye bead she'd kept from an old dress of her grandmother's. They kept everything up here. There would always be a day or a way to use it. Braiding the bead into the bracelet, she finished it with a secure knot and fashioned a loop. At the other end, she used the strands she had left to weave a button at the end so he could button the bracelet on and not have hanging strings. She'd done this for years.

When she'd finished Aidyn's bracelet, she admired her work for a short time, then worked in some of the oil they kept to soften it. Once she was proud of her work, she tucked it into her blouse, hooking it to the strap of the tank top she wore underneath. There was a time she had a bra, but as she grew that one didn't fit anymore, and they didn't have a way to get her another one. Her mom made her tank tops out of some of her dad's old shirts. She added a cinch just under her breasts to hold them in place better.

She'd sleep with it tonight, near her, against her skin. Tomorrow she'd sneak down the mountain and give it to Aidyn. Even if she had to leave it in the basket.

She stood and stretched her back, added a couple of logs to the fire and snuck back to bed. She undressed partially, taking her britches and overshirt off, then slid under the covers and laid her hand over Aidyn's bracelet.

Her other hand, she lay over her lips, remembering his kiss. The way his lips felt against hers was something she just couldn't imagine. She'd been kissed before. Not like Aidyn kissed her, though. When she was younger, there were about six other kids up here at the time, all around her same age, they experimented. The boys were especially interested in experimenting. They always wanted to touch the girls. There were three boys and three girls, and those boys were always trying to touch her breasts.

They were rough and not very romantic about any of it, though. Then one of the girls—Amelia, she was the girl Elena liked the best—giggled and lifted her shirt one night when the six of them were together. They were down by the stream where they had a little nook carved out for them to be unseen.

Oh, she'll never forget the way those boys looked at Amelia. They touched her breasts and squeezed excitedly. One of the boys asked Amelia, "Can I kiss your titties?" Amelia had laughed and said, "Sure." He did. He kissed her breasts and she said, "Oh, that feels good." Then he sucked one in his mouth, and she moaned. Elena never forgot the sound she made. After that, Amelia took turns going to the nook alone with the boys. One at a time.

Amelia got pregnant by one of those boys. She didn't know who. She was only fourteen years old, which up here wasn't that young. They encouraged the girls to get pregnant and have babies. But it didn't work that well for Amelia. She died having that baby and there was something wrong with the baby and it died about a week later.

About a year later, Elena's hormones kicked in and she fancied one of the older boys up there. Davey. She was fifteen he was twenty. He had muscles and when he took his shirt off, he was fine. He saw her looking at him one day and walked over to her, his eyes never left hers. He was like a cat stalking prey.

"You like what you see, Elena?"

She could only whisper, "Yes."

He wrapped his arms around her and pulled her tightly to his body. He barely kissed her. A couple of times on her lips, but it was hard and impersonal.

He half carried her, she half walked backwards, into the woods and he said, "You want to know what it feels like to have sex?"

Her mouth was dry, but he was so handsome. She nodded.

He put her hand on the bulge in his trousers and she

rubbed it. He pushed his hips into her hand as she stroked him, said it felt so good.

"Let me make you feel good too, Elena. Take your clothes off."

She swallowed but she couldn't stop herself. She'd never felt good in a sexual way.

She took her clothes off and he stared at her. "Whew, honey I'd never know that body was under them baggy-ass clothes."

He dropped to his knees before her and licked her. There. She was shocked and gasped. He grabbed her hips and licked her again. Her legs shook and feelings like she'd never had zinged through her body. He laughed. "No one has done this to you, Elena?"

"No."

"Oh, this is gonna be fun."

He laid her on the ground and crawled over the top of her. He put his penis down there and pushed in. Pain shot through her, and she tried to pull away, but he held her in place. "Hang on. It gets better. Just relax a minute and it'll be good."

After a minute Davey started pulling out and pushing back into her. It didn't feel good like he promised. He started grunting and panting and got rough and then he stiffened and groaned and fell flat on top of her.

She swallowed and blinked furiously to keep from crying. She didn't understand what the fuss was all about, and she never went near Davey ever again. She went to church the next day and begged God to forgive her and please don't let her be pregnant. Grateful when her period came, she set about learning to brew elixir and stayed away from boys.

This was the first time in all these years that a man

had caught her attention and even though that first time was awful, she couldn't help but wonder what it would be like to make love to Aidyn. He was kinder than any other man she'd ever known. His kiss was soft and his tongue felt so good in her mouth. His body pressed against hers excited her in ways she'd never been excited before. She drifted off to sleep kissing Aidyn in her mind.

17

Aidyn loaded the magazine for his gun and aimed at the target. This time he was shooting at twenty feet. Firing off eleven rounds in quick succession, he stopped and assessed his aim. A little low, but not bad.

He'd grown up with parents who ensured he and his sister knew how to shoot. Proper etiquette on all things firearms. Know how to clean your gun, how to hold it, never, ever, ever point it at anyone or anything unless you intend to destroy it.

He was the sharpshooter in his Army unit. He'd shot competition as a young boy, a teenager, and a young man. His mom owned a gun range and taught lessons and there was nothing in his childhood that didn't revolve around guns and proper handling of guns.

It was how he'd managed to shoot Everett Howard in the melee of people milling about when he'd tried breaking into the cabin to harm Lara and Tate. The puzzle was, who shot Faye, Keaton Bennit's lover? And who shot Keaton Bennit? It was one of the BRR, but no one was talking. And that right there was a mystery. Why didn't they care? They wouldn't let the townsfolk perform an investigation on "their" land, so as to who shot him, that person was still running around up there, guilty but unpunished. And he'd shot Faye too. One of their own. Why wasn't Kent pissed off about that? Both of his parents gone.

There was the possibility that Kent shot them himself. Though to what end Aidyn couldn't figure. Unless he was tired of the things his father had done to them.

Stowing his practice weapon, holstering his daily weapon, he cleaned up his area to leave the gun range as he found it. Aidyn picked up his shell casings and tossed them in the five-gallon collection pail which they sent off to be refilled and used as practice bullets.

Meandering back through the garage, he saw Spencer entering from outside.

"Hey there, what's up?"

Spencer pointed out of the garage, "Look at the smoke up on the mountain. It seems like they're brewing again."

"They are. Craig wants to sell a second batch to pay for the taxes."

"How do you know that?"

"I've been sneaking around."

Spencer's eyes widened. "You'd better be careful Aid. You know they'd love nothing more than to kill you and dump you on the road."

He took a deep breath. "I know. But it's our job to know what they're doing up there and I'm going to do my job."

"Does Tate know?"

"Yeah."

Spencer nodded. "I'm on with you tonight. Tate's taking Lara out for dinner and some party Shianne is throwing."

"Why aren't you going? Didn't you and Shianne have fun at the Bourbon Ball?"

Spencer shrugged. "It was alright, but we're not that compatible."

Aidyn chuckled. "Okay. I'll be ready in about a half hour or so."

They entered the house together where Adelaide sat at the counter talking to their new cook and housekeeper, Helissa.

"So, you actually like cooking?"

Helissa was middle-aged but slender. Her hair was dark with gray streaks running through it, though she had it pulled back and twisted into a bun at the nape of her neck.

"Yes. I enjoy cooking. I've been doing it my entire life. I take it you don't like cooking."

Addy shrugged. "Not really. But then I've never really cooked. We've always had a cook at home. My mom's a doctor and worked a fair amount and my dad is an operative like us here, so there were times he was gone too."

Helissa nodded and continued to cut carrots. She turned as they entered. "Hello. Supper will be ready in thirty minutes."

Aidyn nodded and grinned at Adelaide. "Did you come up with a name yet?"

"I'm still waiting for your input."

Aidyn waved his hand, "Feel free to go one without me. I'm not creative in that way. My kids one day will be named One, Two, and Three."

This made the room laugh. All of them.

Addy shook her head. "I hope your wife will be more creative than that. Poor little kids."

He shrugged and went back to his bedroom to pack his laptop case. He'd purchased Elena a pair of fingerless gloves today that had a mitten top she could pull over her bare fingers if she needed to warm them. He wanted to give them to her tonight. Hopefully she'd be able to come down the mountain, otherwise on his way home he'd tuck them under the vines at the big tree.

Pulling his laptop case strap over his shoulder, he moved through the house. He still enjoyed the way it was set up. Their rooms were all separated throughout the house. So that when they married, like Tate and Lara, and they'd want to live on site for a while, there'd be some privacy. His room was at the east side of the house, which suited him because it was closest to the foot of the mountain. He wondered if Elena would ever come here. He stopped in the dining room at the thought of her sitting at the table with him and it gave his stomach a flutter. Shaking his head, he turned and walked through the kitchen and out to his truck to stow his laptop with his gift for Elena.

He swallowed as he laid his hand over the case where her gloves were tucked away. His feelings were so jumbled up about her. He barely knew her but she called to him. He knew she lived a hard life and that hurt his heart; he lived in this nice home while she lived in a cabin in the mountains. Not that that was bad, but it wasn't plush.

Her clothing was rudimentary but clean. Her hair and skin were soft and that was the contrast. She lived a simple life but didn't act like it. And she smelled like lavender and...more.

And he liked kissing her. Her lips were soft and molded to his perfectly. Her body fit his in all the right ways. But he knew he had to be careful, so she wasn't a target up there. He didn't know if she had a way to protect herself.

18

Elena strode to the brewing area in the morning and began setting up the still they used. It had been pieced together over the years as parts broke on it. It worked and did what it was supposed to do. Basically, she'd take the mixture she'd boiled down yesterday and pour it into the still, bits at a time. She'd heat it up and boil it then as it cooled the condensation and vapor would be captured. She didn't have a copper pot, which was ideal, so she used copper components to remove the sulfur-based compounds from her elixir.

It was painstaking the way they did it. Kent had told her they had modern apparatuses they used in larger facilities in the outside world. She didn't have access to that, so she maintained the old-fashioned way, the way she was taught, and hopefully Craig would always find her useful. If not, she'd need to find a way off the mountain and survive differently.

She poured some of her mixture into the still then started the fire under it to begin the boil. She felt eyes on her but refused to look around. Then she heard his voice.

"Morning, Elena. Glad to see you started this morning."

She took a deep breath and plastered on a smile before turning to see Craig standing a few yards away from her.

"Morning. Need to get an early start so the first batch can be finished later today."

She didn't wait for him to answer and made herself look busier than she was. The way he stared gave her the creeps.

She scooped more of the liquid from the large kettles into a pail and slowly poured it into the still as it heated. Craig watched her for a long time.

Finally, Theresa approached from her right. "Morning, Elena. What can I help you with today?"

"Morning, Theresa. I have laundry to do today if you don't mind."

"Not at all. I've got some at home too. I'll do it all together."

"Thank you. And the meals you made yesterday were delicious. Thank you. I never could make a biscuit."

Theresa smiled. "Mama insisted I learn."

Theresa strode from the brewing area, which was set aside from the main courtyard. She watched Theresa turn toward her cabin and made a mental note just where she was out of sight. Craig watched her for a while, then turned and stomped over to the main meeting hall they'd constructed a couple of years ago. Most of his work was conducted there. His wife, Hanalore, was seldom seen out of the cabin. The rumor that ran hot around the mountain was she hadn't managed to get pregnant, and she was embarrassed. With all of Craig's blustering on about having kids and keeping their population thriving, he and Hanalore hadn't managed that for themselves.

Elena took a deep breath and listened as the liquid in the still began to boil. This was the part that took a bit of precision. She'd have to manage the boil so it didn't boil too hot and evaporate all the liquid too fast. She needed it to boil steadily for the condensation and vapors to rise through the tubing of the still so she could collect it.

This was the part that was hard to teach. It took patience and few of them up here had that. There were days she didn't have it. Today was one of those days.

She thought about Aidyn and how she'd manage to get down there tonight. Her current plan was to take a bucket with her to collect good soil. Usually this time of year, she replanted the seeds she'd collected from the various plants or replanted those she'd propagated. This kept their supply healthy and it got her away from camp.

Yes, that's how she'd do it tonight.

The fire needed to slow, so she took a shovel from the edge of her brew shelter and dispersed the logs to slow it down.

She stood and saw Craig watching once again. She smiled weakly and continued to work the fire. Then she heard his boots crunching on the ground as he neared and her stomach twisted.

"Maybe you need an apprentice, Elena. Someone to help you. This is hard work."

"It's good work though and I enjoy it."

"Why is it you haven't married and had kids, Elena?"

She froze for a moment, then continued shoveling the hot wood and coals to the fireplace in the corner.

"I've never had an interest in anyone up here I guess."

"Hmm."

"I can help you with that. Some of the young ones are coming to an age where they need to settle down."

"You must have other things to do that are more important than playing matchmaker."

She tried chuckling but it sat heavy in her throat and her stomach threatened to revolt.

"There's nothing more important than keeping our numbers up, Elena. I've stressed this for years."

She swallowed the lump in her throat and tried to smile once again.

"Yes, you have."

Luckily at that moment, the vapors began turning to enough liquid to drip into the glass jug under the spout and she busied herself with that.

Grateful when Craig walked away, she sucked in some deep breaths and stretched her shoulders to calm herself.

After the first batch of brew was distilled, Elena began the second batch of the day. Repeating all she'd done and keeping herself busy so no one would talk to her.

As night fell, she sat in her brewing area, near the fire and watched as the last few drops of liquid dripped into her glass jar. Once it finished, she pushed a cork firmly into the end of the jar, dispersed the fire and carried the jar to her cabin for safe keeping.

After entering the cabin, the only light the glow from the fire, her mom sleeping in the back, Elena tucked the jar into a chest and locked it. Then slipped out of the cabin and around the back. She had a wooden bucket she used to collect soil, but her destination was the base.

Slipping quietly down the mountain, she warmed her hands in her pockets here and there. She'd felt embarrassed last night when Aidyn touched her hand, and it was cold. His was warm and strong and powerful.

She crossed the road near the base and watched for Aidyn. Then she heard a sound. "Psst."

She turned toward the sound and saw him crouched in the brush. She neared him and the second they were close enough, he kissed her. They remained crouched down, the brush higher than their heads in this section, but his lips touched hers and his hands held her head.

When their lips pulled apart he whispered, "I couldn't wait to see you."

"Me too."

His hands sought hers, but she pulled back slightly and rubbed them together. "I'm sorry. I don't want you to feel the cold from me."

He took her hands in his and pushed them against his chest. "I'll warm you."

She stared into his eyes. The lights from the base illuminated the sky around them, though they remained in the shadows. But she saw the clear hazel color as he stared into her eyes and she wanted to commit it to memory.

He whispered, "Did you have a hard day?"

She swallowed as she thought about it. "Weird, I guess."

"In what way?" He stared into her eyes and she saw sincerity in them.

But she felt stupid saying anything. "It doesn't matter."

His hands framed her face. "It does matter."

They stared in silence for a few moments. She took a deep breath. "Craig hinted that he wants me to marry and have kids."

His eyes rounded. "What?"

She felt his fingers shake and he pulled back slightly and took both of her hands in his. She wasn't sure what to do with his reaction, so she said nothing.

"Please explain this to me, Elena." His voice was soft, but his expression changed. His brows furrowed and his lips, just moments before were so soft, now drew a hard line across his handsome face.

She swallowed. "He feels it's important to keep our population thriving. I'm twenty-eight now. I'm fortunate that Everett left me alone to brew elixir and propagate plants. But Craig is a whole different man."

"Do they..." He heaved out a breath. "Does that happen up there? Forced marriage?"

"I've seen it happen."

He gasped but continued to hold her hands.

"My God, it never occurred to me."

19

His head spun around and his vision faded. It never occurred to him that Craig would intend to keep their population thriving and robust. It made sense though. He'd scarcely thought about their population aging out.

"Why is he focusing on you now?"

She shrugged and he saw her lips tremble. "I don't know. He's been staring at me a lot and I'm trying not to let my paranoia get the best of me. I don't think he knows I've been coming down here. But I'm not sure. He needs me to finish this brew right now."

"Do you think after the brew you won't be safe?"

She sucked her lips into her mouth and looked away. "I don't know."

He saw Spencer leave the trailer and begin a patrol. He took her hand in his, "We can go down to the container now, Spencer won't see us on camera." He stood but bent over, "Stay low."

He navigated the tall brush, following the same path

he'd brought here and reminded himself to use a different path tomorrow.

At the bottom of the hill and near the site, he stopped and looked around. Seeing no movement, he pulled Elena to the container and eased them inside.

Once inside, he pulled her to his body and held her close. Her arms wrapped around his waist, and he closed his eyes. Her breathing slowed and he knew they didn't have long.

"I brought you these." He pulled the gloves from his back pocket and held them out to her.

"Oh, these are wonderful Aidyn." She whispered.

She touched them, ran her fingers over them, admired them and pulled them to her chest and hugged them.

"Honey, put them on. Your fingers are so cold."

She slid them over her fingers then looked at the top that hung off the back.

He chuckled. "You can pull it over and keep your fingers warm. When you need to work, you can pull them back."

He showed her the mitten's use and she smiled. "I've never seen something like this."

He kissed her fingers. "Now you have."

She tilted her head back to look into his eyes. "Thank you, Aidyn. They are beautiful."

"You're welcome." He hugged her close again then kissed her lips. "Elena, you need to tell me if you are in danger. Immediately, so I can help you."

"You will be killed if you go up there Aidyn. I can't sacrifice you for myself."

"Come down here. I'll help you. You'll be safe down here."

"I can't. My mom is sick. Her heart is bad. She struggles to move around. I can't leave her up there. They'll let her die. And she'll be all alone. I can't do that."

"We'll help her down here."

"Aidyn!"

He froze. "Spencer's looking for me. Stay right here."

He stepped from the container and moved toward Spencer. "Hey, what's up?"

"There you are. I didn't know what happened to you."

"I thought I saw something up there, then I heard something hit the container. I opened it up to check, but I didn't see anything in there."

"Okay. Just wanted to make sure you were okay."

"All good. I'll just close up the container and I'll be right in."

"Roger that. I have to use the head."

Spencer ambled toward the trailer and Aidyn slipped inside the container.

"Okay, I'll have to slip you out of here before he starts looking at the security cameras."

"Okay."

He kissed her lips again, needing one last feel and taste of her. Then he remembered the cookie in his jacket pocket. "I also brought you this."

He handed her the cookie and she smiled brightly. "Oh, thank you."

She pulled open her jacket, and the shirt she wore and worked at something. Finally, she pulled out a piece of leather.

She smiled. "Put your hand out."

His brows furrowed then smoothed. "Okay."

She wrapped the leather around his wrist and fastened it. "I made this for you. It's not much, but my dad tanned the deer hide and I braided it last night."

"It's beautiful." What he could see of it in the dim light.

"I slept with it against my chest last night. I wanted to absorb my love into it."

A flood of emotion erupted in his chest and his eyes watered. His breathing caught and when he opened his mouth to say something, nothing could come out.

He sniffed, then swallowed. His voice came as a whisper. "I can feel it."

He kissed her again. Long and slow and deep.

"Tomorrow, if you can come down, I'll pick you up by the tree. Jump in my truck and we'll go somewhere so we won't be seen. Same time."

"Okay." She sounded breathless.

He pulled her toward the opening in the container, then quickly slid out and moved to the brush. He held her close and tried infusing his feelings into his hug. Whatever they were.

She lifted on her toes and kissed him quickly, then disappeared into the brush silently.

He stood watching. Listening. Controlling his breathing. Willing his heart to slow its beating.

Turning toward the site, he shook his head and sniffed once more.

He closed the container door and ambled to the trailer. His heart felt too heavy to carry and he felt like he had the weight of the world on his shoulders. Then Elena's words came to him, *"Craig hinted that he wants me to marry and have kids."* That made his guts roll. What a horrible life for a woman to be forced to marry and bear someone's children she didn't love. And how did that affect the children?

He always knew his mother loved him and when he

was five, his dad came into the picture and from that first moment on, he knew his dad loved him. And he knew his parents loved each other.

He clomped up the metal steps to the trailer and opened the door to see Spencer staring at the cameras on his computer.

Spencer turned and stared at him but said nothing. A shiver skittered down his spine. Eventually, he'd have to tell his teammates about Elena. Tate already knew they had exchanged notes, but he didn't know that their relationship had grown to more. Though he couldn't even explain what their relationship was except he wanted to spend more time with her. He wanted to make love to her. He wanted to protect her. He wanted more time with her. He wanted...

20

Elena scooted up the mountain as quickly as she could. It was easier, thanks to Aidyn and the gloves he'd given her. She didn't have to keep putting her hands in her pockets to warm them.

She fisted her hands and felt the warm leather of the gloves and her heart skipped a beat. He wanted to help her. He wanted to pick her up tomorrow night in his truck and go somewhere they could be alone. It excited her to think about it. Alone, where they didn't have to worry about anyone seeing them together. Her heart fluttered again.

Something snapped and she froze. Footsteps. She had to put soil in her bucket and fast.

She stopped and pulled her gloves off and slipped them into her jacket pocket. Using the little hand shovel her dad had made, she scooped some soil from the area she was in and began filling her bucket.

Her mouth dried out and her heartbeat raced. Fear skittered down her spine as she dug furiously for nice fresh soil.

Finally, she felt as though she had enough to explain herself and stood. She listened for movement but heard none, so she made her way up her path toward the cabin.

A man stepped from the woods and blocked her path. She gasped and blinked as her eyes adjusted.

"What are you doing out here this late at night, Elena?"

"Liam? Is that you?"

"Yes. Not sure what it matters."

"It doesn't. I guess."

"Now, answer my question."

Liam Price was one of Craig Howard's council members and he loved his new role.

She lifted her bucket. "I'm gathering soil so I can start seeds and plants inside."

"Why do you come way out here?"

"The soil is better. It's virgin soil, sort of. No chemicals have been in it. The plants rot and fertilize it and it makes the best potting soil for new seeds."

Liam stared at her for a long time. "Why so late at night?"

She cleared her throat. "In case you haven't noticed, I've been brewing all day. Yesterday and today and I will be for a couple of weeks. When do you think I should do this? Should I tell Craig the brew will have to wait because you don't want me out here in my spare time?"

"I didn't say I didn't want you out here. I was just asking."

She mustered the courage to brush past him in a huff. "Good night, Liam."

Her heart pounded in her chest as she waited to see what his reaction would be. But one thing was certain, he'd be watching for her now. She'd have to be extra careful tomorrow.

Relief washed over her when he didn't follow her, and she finally allowed herself a deep breath.

Setting the bucket of dirt on the stoop of her cabin, she slipped inside and locked the door.

She laid her forehead on the door for a few moments and let her breathing return to a slower cadence.

"Elena?"

She turned to see her mom's eyes open, looking at her. "Yes, Mama, it's me."

"Is everything alright?"

"Yes, Mama." She took her jacket off and hung it on the hook by the door. She hung her apron next.

"Are you sure?"

"Yes. Liam just scared me outside. I'm better now."

"How did he scare you?"

She walked toward the bedroom. "He jumped out at me. That's all."

Her mom sat up, her lips quivered.

"Things are getting scary here, Elena."

"What do you mean?"

Fear skittered up her spine as she sat on the edge of her bed and watched her mom compose herself.

"Theresa told me Craig wants you to marry."

"How does she know that?"

"Apparently she overheard him talking in the meeting compound yesterday to the other men."

She swallowed to keep from vomiting. She pulled her shirt away from her body to cool herself down. Her armpits grew damp.

Lowering her voice, she leaned closer to her mom. "Mama. Aidyn will help us get away from here."

Her mom gasped and her hands flew to her mouth.

"You've been meeting him."

She didn't respond. There was no need. "Elena. You'll get us in trouble."

"I don't want to, Mama. But I sure don't want to marry one of these dogs up here. And I sure as hell don't want to have their brats. They're all like wild rutting animals up here and I won't have it. Craig encourages it to keep the population up."

Tears fell on her mom's cheeks. She whispered, "Aidyn will help us."

Her mom shook her head. "No." She choked back a sob. "Don't do it. It'll cause trouble. A war. They'll hunt him. They'll hunt you both down."

"I'm not leaving up here without you, but I'll not be tied to one of these animals either."

Her mom's hands shook as she tried straightening her blankets.

"I can't leave here. I'll only hold you back."

"We'll figure it out. I'm not leaving you up here, and I believe we're safe until the brewing's done. So, I have a couple of weeks to figure it out. In the meantime, you say nothing. And, just in case Theresa is spying for Craig, you don't let on anything to her. Okay?"

Her mom sniffled and nodded.

"Say it, Mama."

"I won't say anything."

Her mom laid back down and pulled the covers to her chin.

"Elena?"

"Yes, Mama."

"I'll just say this." She took a deep breath. "Whatever you decide to do, I support you. But I do urge you to use caution, set up a plan for the future. When I'm gone, you'll be alone."

She swallowed and nodded. "Okay."

Elena stood and put two more logs in the fireplace. She pulled her new gloves from the pocket of her jacket and looked at them.

They were leather but had fur on the inside. The mitten top was lined with fur and it was so soft.

She turned them over in her hand so she could see them in the light of the fireplace. A tear fell on them and she swiped it off quickly so it wouldn't stain.

Brushing the tears from her cheeks, she tried thinking what it would be like up here with one of these men rutting away on top of her and she wanted to throw up. Emotionless and nasty just like with Davey. She never wanted to have to go through anything like that ever again.

Aidyn parked at the construction site and took a deep breath. He hoped Elena would be able to break away tonight. But first and foremost, she had to be safe.

As he neared the construction office a loud whistle caught his attention. A flare lit the sky, and he dove behind his truck the instant he realized what was happening.

The explosion rocked the ground around him. Spencer ran out of the construction trailer and he called over to him.

"Spencer! Get down."

Spencer turned toward him and dove behind the truck with Aidyn.

"What the fuck?"

"They're launching explosives."

"Sonofabitch."

"Yeah."

The whistle of another incoming explosive rent the air and they both ducked their heads as the projectile landed.

The ground once again shook, but this time, the grotesque sounds of the new partially erected metal communication tower screeched and groaned before bending over.

He and Spencer peered around his truck and watched the tower crash to the ground, half landing on one of the containers.

They stared at the mangled mess of metal and wire as the dust and debris cleared.

He pulled his phone from his pocket and tapped the screen on Tate's picture.

"What the hell was that?" Tate answered.

"They've begun launching explosives at us. The last one hit the south communication tower."

"Fuck!"

His eyes scanned the area in the hills for any sign of movement.

Tate took a deep breath. "Are you and Spencer injured?"

"No. We're both fine. Luckily, I heard the whistle of it flying through the air and took cover."

"I'll be right there."

"Roger."

The sounds of motors fading up into the hills reached his ears.

"Fuckers are leaving."

Spencer cleared his throat. "Those bastards are going too far."

"Agreed."

Sparks flew from the exposed wires. Some of them were hooked to power for tools and equipment to be used in building the tower.

Spencer stood. "I'll cut the power."

"Roger. I'm going around the back and will check out the damage."

Spencer left and he heaved out a deep breath before making his way around the front of his truck and to the back area of the construction site. In case they were watching, he'd stay in the shadows. They'd been instructed to wear their flak jackets and he was happy right now to have it.

Moving between the footings for one of the back buildings and the storage containers, he watched the hills more than the ground. The instant he heard incoming, he'd dive behind one of these containers and hope for the best.

A few steps more and he could see the damage directly. It was nothing more than a tangled mess of metal and wire. The arcing stopped and he ventured closer to the base of the communication tower. A gunshot rang out and a bullet hit the ground a foot from where he stood. He ran for cover behind one of the containers, his weapon drawn.

He heard the trailer door close and pulled his phone from his pocket. He tapped Spencer's number and the instant he answered, "Where are..."

"Get down. Shots fired."

He heard Spencer run for cover, but his eyes were focused on the hills and the direction of the shot.

He saw the brush move and took aim. Firing off three shots he waited. The brush stopped moving, but he knew from this distance using a handgun, he'd hit nothing but ground.

He put his phone back to his ear. "Spencer, where are you?"

"I'm walking along the back of the containers toward the tower. Is that where you are?"

"Affirmative."

He pocketed his phone once more and decided to test the area. He stepped from behind the container just as two trucks pulled into the lot. Rather than watch the trucks, he watched the brush to see if it moved.

It did. Toward the mountain, so whoever was up there decided to take off as soon as support arrived.

Moving closer to the tower, he saw remnants of the explosive they used. It was similar to the one they'd used yesterday. Pieces of the piping they'd stolen from the construction site previously, filled with screws, nuts and bolts and an accelerant added. Except now they were launching them.

Tate and Henry neared him. "Are you alright?" Tate asked.

"Yeah. Whoever launched the explosives also took a shot at me."

He toed the ground where the bullet hit and saw a fragment of the shell casing in the dirt. He bent and picked it up.

"Looks like a 28mm rifle bullet."

Tate looked up into the brush then to the ground. He took a deep breath. "Was that meant for you or was he just firing?"

Aidyn looked at his friend. "I think it was meant for me. I was standing right here." He moved to the spot where he'd been. "I jumped back to the containers and took cover."

Tate nodded.

Henry looked around at the tower with Spencer, assessing everything that had been damaged.

He took a deep breath and gathered his thoughts. His body began shaking slightly, the rush of adrenaline leaving as fast as it rushed in. Tate slapped him on the shoulder. "Take off, Aid. I've got this for tonight."

"I'm alright."

"No. Get your head on straight. Drink some water, maybe work out a bit to release the adrenaline. Between Henry and me, we've got you covered."

He took a deep breath. "Okay."

Long strides to his truck helped him to metabolize the adrenaline and his thoughts went to Elena. He wouldn't have to make up an excuse to pick her up tonight. That was good. The guilt had been weighing on him the whole day. And as bad as that was, he still couldn't wait to spend time with Elena.

He hopped in his truck and left the parking lot. As he neared their spot, he slowed, then decided to leave her a note.

The parking lot across the street offered him the best vantage point to wait for her. Pulling a small notebook from the glove box, he wrote, "I'm across the street. Black truck."

He ripped the paper from his notebook and jumped from his truck. Opening the tonneau cover he reached into the toolbox he carried in the back and pulled a nail and a hammer from inside. Striding across the street with his note and the hammer, he found a downed branch and hammered it into the ground in the spot where Elena's basket usually sat. He pushed the note over the stick, leaving it barely visible and slightly indented into the vines.

Striding across the street to his truck, he replaced his hammer in his toolbox, closed the tonneau cover and jumped back into the driver's seat. Checking the clock on his phone he saw he was about an hour early.

He lifted the bottle of water from the cup holder and removed the lid. His hands still shook as he lifted the water to his lips, but the cool liquid felt fantastic sliding down his throat.

A knock on his window startled him awake. Elena stood at the passenger window staring in at him.

Quickly unlocking the door, he watched her look around before opening the door. She climbed up into his truck and froze. Her eyes stared at the computer screen on the dashboard. His radio had been turned low so he could sleep while he waited for her. But the words scrolling across the screen caught her attention. "The name of the song. The station that I'm listening to and the temperature."

She grinned. "I can read."

"I know you can. I also know you can write."

She smiled. Her beautiful green eyes almost glittered as her expression changed from mirth to seriousness. They stared at each other. His heart beat rapidly in his chest as her tongue poked out and wet her lips.

He couldn't look away. His left hand reached over and pulled her head to his. Their lips touched and he felt the electricity run through his body. Her breathing hitched and his lips moved over hers eager to fully taste her.

Her right hand cupped his cheek, then slid back and tangled in his hair at his nape.

He enjoyed her lips, her tongue, her scent until he needed air. Pulling back only enough to drag breath into his lungs, he whispered. "We need to go somewhere more private."

"Okay."

He started the truck. "Buckle your seatbelt, Elena."

She cocked her head to the side. "What's that?"

His eyes widened. "Here, let me help you."

He reached across her and pulled at the seatbelt hanging on the other side of her. He pulled it around her and clipped it in place. "Seatbelt. To protect you if we have an accident."

"Oh." She sounded breathy when she responded, and he wanted to make her breathy again.

He pulled back slightly. "Have you ever ridden in a vehicle before?"

She shook her head and looked at her hands in her lap.

He lifted her chin with two fingers under it. "No need to be embarrassed. I'll be careful so you don't get scared."

"Okay." Her eyes stared into his and his heart—wow. It synced to the rhythm of the rock song on his radio.

He sat back and started his truck. His brain had scrambled around all day trying to decide where they could go. A hotel seemed seedy and anticipatory. He wanted to talk to her. He wanted to spend time while not having to look over his shoulder the whole time. He wanted to get to know her.

In the end, he settled on the old house they had just moved out of. They still held the lease until the end of the month and it would be private.

He drove the backstreets, making sure they weren't being followed and he glanced at Elena many times as they drove. She looked out the windows, her eyes rounded in amazement.

"What do you call this music?" she asked.

He stared at her a moment, then smiled. "Rock. It's actually country rock, I suppose."

She didn't respond.

"Do you listen to music up on the mountain?"

"Sometimes. Some of the people up there have great voices. They sit around the fire in the evenings sometimes and sing. But it's mostly hymns."

"Do you have church up there?"

She smiled softly. "Yes. Every Sunday."

He turned into the driveway and tapped the garage door. Driving into the garage, Elena clutched the armrest and froze.

"It's okay, honey."

Her eyes darted to his then to the garage as he stopped. He tapped the button to close the door and exited the truck. He strode around to the passenger side and helped her step down to the ground.

"Where is this?"

"This is the house we used to rent before we remodeled the sewing factory and moved in there."

"Okay."

He took her hand in his and led her to the door at the side of the garage. He peered out before stepping out, making sure no one was lurking around.

He led Elena from the garage to the back door. He opened the door for her to step inside before him. He secured the locks. When he turned to her, she stared at the kitchen, her mouth open in amazement.

He swallowed to moisten his throat, and to remove the lump that had lodged inside. It dawned on him that she'd never seen a kitchen like this.

"Tell me what you want to know."

Her eyes landed on his and held for a moment, before her lips turned up into a soft smile. "I want to know it all. What is all of this?"

He moved into the kitchen and opened the refrigerator. "This is a refrigerator. It keeps food items cold. The freezer keeps food frozen."

Elena stood in front of the open refrigerator door and stared inside.

He moved to the stove. "This is the stove and oven."

Then moved to the counter. "This is the sink." He turned on the faucet and she slowly approached. She put her hand under the stream of water and giggled. His heart fluttered and his excitement grew. He wanted to show her everything.

He took her hand and moved into the dining room and through to the living room. He turned on the television and she gasped as her hands flew to her mouth.

"This is television. The people are actors and actresses. They act out stories for us to watch. Unless we're watching the news; those people just tell us what's going on in the world."

Her head slowly turned to him. "The whole world?"

"The whole world." He pulled his phone from his pocket. "This is a minicomputer, I guess. I know Kent has one or one similar to it. Have you ever seen it?"

She shook her head. "He told me there's a thing called a shower."

A grin spread across his face. "I can show you one."

Taking her hand in his, he pulled her to the bathroom and turned on the light. "This is a shower."

He turned on the water, then pulled up the lever to start the spray and she giggled. "Oh wow."

She eased forward and put her hand under the stream of water and giggled again.

He stepped aside and turned the water in the sink on.

"Why do you have two waterspouts?"

"We call them faucets. This one is if you are washing your hands after you use the toilet."

"Toilet?"

He pulled the door closed and exposed the toilet hiding behind it. "This is where we go to the bathroom."

"Oh."

He pushed the handle down to flush the water and she jumped. "Cleans the bowl after."

She leaned down and watched the water swirl then disappear. The look on her face when she stood was adorable.

"Wow."

He grinned at her innocence and wonder of it all. He'd grown up with all of this and it seemed like nothing. To her? It was a wonder.

"I want to know about you Elena. What do you use to shower? How do you get water to your house? What does your everyday look like?"

22

She looked into his eyes and didn't see mocking or insult.

"I carry water from the stream."

He took her hand and walked her into the living room. They sat on a comfortable bench-type thing he called a sofa. They turned toward each other and talked. It seemed like hours. He asked about her life. About her mom. About her mom's illness. He touched her all the time. His fingers, while work-roughened and strong, were gentle when he brushed her cheeks.

His hands held hers. And they kissed. Often. She wanted more.

He looked into her eyes, "What time do you have to be back?"

"Before dawn."

His eyes rounded, then he grinned. He reached his arm around her waist and pulled her onto his lap. She straddled his legs, he rested his head on the back of the sofa and stared up into her eyes. Leaning down, she kissed his lips. She tasted him as he did her. She pressed her breasts to his chest and felt him harden between her legs.

Her hands dug into his hair and her fingers roamed around his scalp. He sunk lower onto the sofa, and she rotated her hips enjoying the friction between them.

He held her hips on either side and pushed her down onto him firmly. She moaned. This was nothing like Davey.

"Aidyn," she whispered.

He whispered back, but his voice was raspy. "Elena."

She whimpered. She wanted to hear her name come out of his mouth as they had sex. She wanted to have sex with him. Now.

Her fingers fumbled with his shirt, pulling it from his pants. Her palms pressed against the skin of his abdomen, then slid up over his nipples. She liked the inhale of breath he took when she played with his nipples. Rotating her palms over the hardened nubs caused him to lift his hips into her core.

"Aidyn. I want to have sex with you."

He chuckled, though it sounded more like a growl, she felt the vibration in her palms against his warm skin.

"Elena. I want that too."

He sat up, cradling her body to his, and walked them through the living room and up the stairs. He entered a room and closed the door, then locked it. He didn't let her down.

He lay her gently on the bed and she reluctantly released her arms from around his neck as he stood. She stared at him as he unbuttoned his pants and let them fall from his hips.

Lifting his shirt, he pulled it over his head and dropped it to the floor. His thumbs tucked into his briefs, and he pushed them down his legs. His thick, hard penis stood and she found herself staring at it. She'd never seen an erect male before. Certainly not like this. Her muscles clenched between her legs, and she felt moisture gather and pushed her legs together.

He licked his lips and she stared at his face. It seemed as though he was undecided about his next step. Then, he untied the tie around her pants and slowly slid them down her legs. He untied her undergarment and slid it down her legs. Her eyes locked onto his face as he stared at her.

He leaned down and lifted her blouse over her head and let it drop with the other clothing they'd both discarded. He leaned down and moved their clothing around, then stood and looked at her.

A slow grin spread across his handsome face and he slowly pushed her legs open, his fingers then circled her privates in a way that no man had ever touched her before. She'd helped herself over time, but someone else pleasuring her—that had never happened.

She gasped as he hit a sensitive spot and he rotated over and over it again. Her breathing became pants, and her skin was hot and sweaty. Fear crawled through her body because she didn't know what was happening to her but she didn't want him to stop. It felt so good.

His soft gravelly voice lulled her. "Come for me, Elena."

Come. Come? What did that mean exactly?

"I don't know how," she managed.

He smiled the most beautiful smile and increased the pressure between her legs. Everything went dark except the white spots that danced before her eyes. Her body stiffened and pressure between her legs built then released as she said his name. "Aidyn."

He stopped rotating but pushed his fingers tightly against her privates as she felt the pressure release.

Blinking away the darkness, her vision returned to see his serene smile as he stared at her. "That was beautiful, Elena."

She swallowed. "What was that?"

His brows rose and he seemed speechless for a moment. "Have you ever had an orgasm before?"

She shook her head.

"Are you a virgin?"

Shaking her head once more, she felt her cheeks heat.

"So you've had sex, but never an orgasm?"

"One..." She cleared her throat. "Once. It wasn't enjoyable."

He crawled over the top of her body, kissing her belly, her breasts, her chest, her neck, and finally her lips as he did. She'd never been kissed in all those places. She didn't know people did that.

His lips kissed her cheek to her ear and he whispered. "To have sex properly, both parties should always have an orgasm at the end. That's what makes it enjoyable. That's why people want to have sex. It should be pleasurable. If I do anything that doesn't bring you pleasure, I want you to tell me."

She swallowed.

He whispered again, "Okay?"

"Yeah."

He kissed his way across her cheek again, stopping at her lips. He kissed her fully. Their lips melted into each other and their tongues danced.

Then he kissed her chin, her neck and continued

kissing across her chest until he kissed one of her nipples. She gasped and he chuckled. Then he sucked her breast into his mouth, and she gasped again. It was warm and the sucking sensation made moisture gather at her privates again. She tried squeezing her legs together, but he was between them.

Lifting his head he stared down at her. "Did that make you wet?"

A burning crawled across her face and tears gathered in her eyes.

He shook his head. "No, Elena. That's not a bad thing."

He swiped his finger slowly from the base of her private area, up through the part he'd massaged before that made her lose her vision. He lifted his finger and held it up for her to see.

"That, sweetheart, is what happens when you're aroused. It's nature's way of lubricating you so when I slide inside of you, it's comfortable."

She swallowed. "Oh."

His lips lifted on one side and he picked up a small package lying on the bed and ripped it open.

"This is a condom. I'm going to roll it on myself to keep us both safe. From disease and from getting pregnant."

"I don't have disease."

"I don't either, honey. But I thought it would make you feel better to know I'm keeping you safe."

His eyes never left hers and she finally nodded. He rolled the protection on, and she couldn't look away. She'd never seen that either.

He leaned down again and positioned his penis between her legs.

"If you ever feel discomfort, you need to tell me. This should be enjoyable."

"Okay."

He entered her body slowly. She felt him the entire way in, until their bodies were joined together completely. She sighed.

He moved then, in and out so slowly she felt every single motion. His lips pressed against hers then he pushed in again. His groans were exciting, and he whispered in her ear, "You feel so fucking good, Elena."

She lifted her knees into the air and it felt like he pushed in further and he groaned. "God."

He rotated his hips once he'd pushed all the way in her and that added pressure to that spot she liked him to touch.

Lifting his upper body off hers, he began moving faster, but his eyes locked on hers. Her hips moved up and down with his and she felt the pleasure rise again. Her hands clamped onto his hips, and she moved him faster into her as the pressure built between her legs again.

She gasped. "Aidyn."

He moved faster still.

"Aidyn."

He pushed into her and she gasped. He pushed in three more times, and he gasped too.

He collapsed on top of her, holding himself up onto his elbows. Their breathing was heavy, their skin was damp.

"Elena. That felt...fantastic."

He lifted his head and stared into her eyes. "Was that pleasurable?" He swallowed. "Did you feel good?"

She laid her hand against his cheek, though his face blurred from the tears that gathered in her eyes.

"Yes. That was pleasurable. I never knew this feeling existed. Ever."

He kissed her lips softly. "I've never felt quite like this either."

She sought the meaning in his eyes, but all she saw was sincerity. They stared at each other for a long time. She didn't want to stop staring at him. Ever.

23

Aidyn lay on his side, his head in his hand and watched Elena as she slept. Her petite face was beautiful in rest. It was always beautiful though. Her dark hair fanned out around her in a cloud of silk.

Gently sliding his forefinger into a curl, he admired the color and the soft texture. He smoothed his thumb over the dark curl and took a deep breath.

Her eyes fluttered open and instantly sought his.

"Hi." Her lips spread into a soft smile.

"Hi." He leaned in and kissed her lips.

Her smile faded. "I think I have to go."

He only nodded because his throat clogged up.

She inhaled a deep breath and let it out slowly.

"Elena, are you safe up there?"

Her lips pressed together, and her eyes looked up at the ceiling.

She swallowed and rolled to her side to face him. "Craig is going to make me marry soon."

It was like a gut punch. His lungs constricted and his stomach twisted into a knot.

When he spoke, it was difficult to push the words out. "How do you know?"

"My mom told me."

He gently turned her face toward his. "Do you want that?"

Tears filled her eyes. She only shook her head.

"When?"

She softly sniffed. "I hope I'm able to finish this brew."

"Let me bring you down here."

"I can't leave my mom, Aidyn. She's sick and they'll let her die."

"I'll bring her, too."

Elena sat up, her hair falling in waves down her bare back. "I have no way to support us. I only know how to make the elixir. I have no other skills. I don't have the money to pay for medical help for my mom."

"Let me make some inquiries. Let me do some research down here. Hold off as long as you can."

"I'll do my best. I promise."

She moved to the edge of the bed and gathered her clothes. Turning to face him, she smiled. "I want to take a shower."

He grinned. "Mind if I join you?"

She shook her head and left the room.

Mentally, he moved the sadness that sat hard in his chest to the side. But time was running out for them, and he needed to figure out what he wanted to do. How he approached all of this with his teammates. And he had to figure out what these heavy feelings were in his chest.

He grabbed his clothes and headed toward the bathroom. The water turned on and he heard Elena gasp in delight. His heart swelled.

He pushed open the door and saw her watching the

water fall from the faucet in wonder. She turned to him, the smile on her face was breathtaking.

"I don't know how to make it come out of there." She pointed to the shower head.

He leaned over and lifted the lever to change the water's path and her mouth fell open.

He tested the temperature with his hand and twisted the handles to warm it up. "You can change how warm or cold it is here." He pulled her hand forward and let the water fall on it. He adjusted the temperature once more and she giggled.

He pulled towels from the cabinet and the shampoo the landlord stored for short-term rental guests. A bar of soap laid near the sink, he grabbed that and stepped into the shower. He held his hand out to Elena and helped her in as well, then closed the shower curtain.

She jumped under the water and let it fall over her body. He enjoyed staring at the rivulets of water as they parted around her breasts and sluiced down her slender body. His fingers brushed over her nipples and her eyes opened. She stepped away from the water and swiped the water from her eyes.

"How about shower sex?" he husked.

"You have sex in the shower?"

"Shower sex is amazing."

He pulled her close, his thickening cock between them as her hands roamed over his body, beginning at his chest, then sliding around to his back, then back to his chest.

He took her hands in his and kissed her fingers, then guided them to his cock. "Touch me here," he growled.

She swallowed, but her hands gently smoothed over his length, tentatively feeling the rigidness of his shaft, the softness of the head of his cock, and then she explored lower and palmed his balls in her hand. He gasped and she jumped back. Pulling her close again, he urged her hands back to where they'd been and closed his eyes as she explored him. He allowed her to play for a while, but the urgency in his body grew too close.

He pulled her hands away gently then kissed her lips.

She smiled. "Show me shower sex."

"Elena."

"Please."

He swallowed the lump in his throat, then turned her to face the wall. He placed her hands on the wall. "Hold yourself up like this."

His lips kissed the shell of her ear as his hands, cupped her breasts and squeezed them in turn. He plucked at her nipples and she arched her back, her butt ramming into his cock. The breath whooshed from his lungs as his arms wrapped around her body and held her still.

Bending his knees, he positioned himself at her entrance and softly whispered in her ear, "I hope you like shower sex, baby."

He pushed into her and she moaned. He thought she did; his groan drowned her out. Pulling out, he pushed back in again and again, the warmth of her body squeezing his cock unlike anything he'd ever experienced.

Keeping one arm around her, he moved his right hand down to massage her clit and she gasped. His lips nipped at her ear as his breathing increased.

"Elena. You feel so fucking good."

She said something he couldn't understand. Her hips moved into his fingers adding pressure and he obliged. She gasped his name, then groaned loudly as her legs began to shake. His hips pushed into her a few more times, the pressure in his balls beyond measure. When he let go her name was on his lips.

His body spasmed and jerked as he continued to hold her. As he softened and pulled away from her sweet body, he wrapped both arms around her and pulled her tightly to his body. Her head fell back to his shoulder and she wrapped her arms around his.

They stood that way for a while, the water still showering down on them.

He turned her in his arms and his lips found hers. He kissed her with everything he had in him. He wanted to convey feelings he couldn't explain. He wanted to feel her feelings for him.

Elena whispered, "I like shower sex too."

24

Aidyn stopped in the parking lot across the street from their tree and her heart felt heavy.

"I'll try and come down tonight."

"Okay. Please be careful."

She tried to smile, but to be honest, she was nervous about getting back to the cabin and how she moved forward from here. The thought of going back up there made her skin crawl. But she didn't know what else to do.

She nodded and opened the door of his truck. She jumped down and looked at him before closing the door.

"Elena?" he said before it closed.

"Yes?"

"Do you have a way to let me know if you need help?"

She slowly shook her head.

"Tonight, I'll bring you a way to contact me."

"Okay."

She scurried across the road, grateful for the cover of darkness. She laid her hand across her roiling tummy and told herself to be strong and not let on she'd been down here.

She disappeared into the woods, picked up the basket she left hidden in the patch of spicebush that was shooting up. It wouldn't bloom for a month or so, but for now it allowed a bit of cover. She picked some of the rosemary and fennel that were blooming close by and filled her basket. The aroma coming from the fresh picked herbs comforted her hurting heart as the familiar washed over her.

She wove quietly through the woods until she came to the path that led to her cabin. Stopping to listen for anyone moving about, she stepped onto the path and effortlessly made her way home. Peering around the side of the cabin, she took a deep breath and stepped to the door. Voices growing closer caught her attention. Instead of listening, she slipped inside and locked the door.

The fire had all but died out, only a few embers left, so she added wood and gently blew on the embers hoping something would catch. She had a sack of dried brush near the fireplace and reached for it when she heard her mom roll over in bed. She froze and waited for her to settle, then changed her mind about making any noise and softly blew on the embers again. Grateful when the wood caught, she sat in silence watching the flames grow and thought of Aidyn.

Her heart flittered around when she thought of him. Her mind danced a jubilee when she remembered how he felt when they made love. He may not have made love, but she did. She loved him. He was a good person. He cared about her. That she was pleasured. That she was warm. That she was safe. He was everything these dogs up here weren't. She wanted that life. With him.

She slid her feet so her knees rose, then crossed her

arms over her knees and laid her head on her arms. Her eyes watched the flames for a long time.

"Elena?"

She lifted her head and blinked. The flames had settled in the fireplace.

"Elena?"

She turned her head to see her mom's worried face staring at her.

"Yes, Mama."

Her mom shuffled to a chair at the table near her and sat. "Elena. Why are you sleeping on the floor?"

She stretched, her muscles sore. She stood, added another log to the fire then sat at the table. "The fire was pretty and I sat to watch it and fell asleep I guess."

"Honey, you're working too hard and then going out at night. You've got to take care of yourself so you don't get sick."

"I'm sorry, Mama. I'll take care of myself. I'll make some chamomile tea right now. Would you like some?"

She didn't wait for an answer. Setting the water kettle on the hook and pushing it into the fire, she pulled two cups from under the counter and busied herself adding chamomile leaves to a steeping bag she'd sewn years ago.

"You were out late."

"Yes."

She quietly inhaled and tried to make the heaviness go away. Setting both cups on the table she lifted the corner of the material on the window to see if there was activity outside. Only one person was up and about. The sun was beginning to rise.

Lifting the water kettle from the hook, she poured hot water into each cup, then sat at the table with her mom.

She wrapped her hands around the cup to warm them and watched the water turn a faint green as the tea steeped.

Her mom's hand lay on one of hers. "Elena, honey. Tell me what's happening."

She lifted her eyes to her mom's and sighed. "We've already talked about this."

"I want you to be safe."

"I'm safe as I can…"

Knocking on the door stopped her. She stood and smoothed her clothing as she moved to the door.

"Who is it?" She asked.

"It's Craig."

She filled her lungs, then looked at her mom, held her finger to her lips. She waited for her mom to nod before lifting the lock on the door.

"Good morning." She feigned cheer as she greeted Craig. Stepping back, she held her hand out to the room. "Please come in."

He stepped in and glanced at the teacups on the table. "I need to speak with you."

"Please sit down. Can I make you some tea?"

He pulled a chair away from the table as she closed the door.

"No. This shouldn't take very long."

Her stomach roiled and she worried she'd vomit the instant he started talking. She added another log to the fire, maybe she could heat him out of her cabin.

She sat and sipped her tea, hoping it would help her tummy settle.

"Elena. I've mentioned this prior to you but we didn't settle on anything specific. However, it's time you marry and have children. I know in the past my father allowed you to stay as you are because you've been the family who kept us in elixir. But we need our numbers to grow, and I've got to keep our group healthy and prosperous."

She took a few deep breaths. She swallowed the lump in her throat and stared him in the eye.

"I don't want to marry and have children. There isn't anyone out there of interest to me."

"There's some younger ones coming along that would be a big help to you and your ma here."

"I don't want a young husband. Or a husband at all."

He stood abruptly. "I demand you marry and have children."

She bit the inside of her cheek. "No." She locked eyes with him. "Thank you."

"How dare you disobey me."

"Since when is it the president's job to force people to marry? Everett never did."

"And our numbers are dwindling."

"Why don't you have children then? It hasn't gone unnoticed that you and Hanalore haven't produced a single child."

His face contorted into something unrecognizable, but she didn't shrink back. She'd rather kill herself than ever allow one of his pigs to hump on her.

Craig raised his hand and smacked her hard across the face.

"You will regret saying that to me."

Her mom stood. "Craig! That is uncalled for."

He stuck his finger in her mom's face. "You shut up."

He turned and stormed out of the cabin, and she hurried to lock the door behind him.

Her heartbeat was erratic. She realized she shouldn't have said anything to him, but she wouldn't obey him in this.

She looked up at her mom and saw the tears rolling down her cheeks. "Elena. This is not good."

25

Aidyn entered the kitchen to a rowdy conversation about the name of their place. He chuckled as Addy said, "Come on you guys. We need to name this place. Get serious about this."

Spencer shrugged. "How about Needle Point, or Mending Box."

"Those aren't bad."

Maya poured herself a cup of coffee. "What about Zipped Tight?"

"That's okay." Addy wrote the names down.

Lara pulled cookies from the oven. "I've come up with The Stitchery, Button Down, and Sown Home."

"I'll write those down."

She pushed the list to the center of the counter, and they leaned over and read the names. Aidyn turned to pour himself a cup of coffee and gather his thoughts. He slept on and off last night. Actually, it was early this morning. He kept thinking about Elena. He wanted to spend more time with her, and this sneaking around rankled him. He wanted to take her out to eat. Show her all the things she had no idea existed out in the real world. And not have to have her sneak down the mountain like a criminal.

Addy called out. "Aidyn, you're the only one who hasn't come up with a single name."

He took a deep breath and let it out slowly. "What about The HOG? Home, Office, and Garage. It's exactly what it is."

Henry chuckled and Spencer punched him in the shoulder. "That's perfect, man."

Lara giggled. "That is cool."

Tate entered the room. "Hey, you okay?"

Aidyn nodded. "Yeah."

Addy circled The HOG on her sheet of paper. "I like this one a lot. Let's see if it sticks."

He glanced at Spencer. "You have a minute?"

"Yeah."

Aidyn strode to the door that led to the backyard and Spencer followed. He swallowed to wet his throat and he took in deep gulps of air to settle his nerves.

He sat on the top of the picnic table so he could look up the mountain. Spencer sat next to him and sipped his coffee.

"Are you okay Aid? You didn't come home till close to three-thirty this morning."

"I need to talk to someone Spence. I know you won't say anything to anyone else and I need your thoughts on something."

"Okay. Sounds kind of heavy."

Aidyn sipped his coffee. "I was with Elena last night."

"Elena?" Spencer turned to look at him, his eyes rounded. "You mean Elena?" He pointed to the mountain.

"Yes. Elena."

"You went up there? Aidyn, you can't be doing that."

"No, she came down here."

"What? How? When?"

He chuckled. "We had it planned. I just wanted to spend time with her. Get to know her better. She's interesting. We talked for hours last night. About our lives and things we want to do in the future. She doesn't want to stay up there but can't leave because of her mom."

"What will she do down here?"

"She's the brewer, Spence."

"The brewer? You mean the elixir? She does that?"

"Yes."

Spencer stared up at the mountain himself and contemplated. Aidyn sipped at his coffee. And when he spoke again, his voice cracked.

"I can't stop thinking about her. I can't get her out of my head."

"Do you love her?"

He turned to look into his friend's eyes. He wasn't mocking, he was serious. "I don't know. I've never been in love before."

"Hmm. I was once. A long time ago. Remember?"

"Yeah. You were head over heels. You kept sneaking out. You wanted to be with her all the time. You kept talking about her. You were with her almost every night."

He froze and turned to stare up at the mountain again. "Shit."

Spencer reared back and laughed. He slapped him on the shoulder. "Man, you're in love with a mountain girl."

Aidyn let that sink in a bit. Then dropped his head. "She might be in danger. Craig Howard wants her to marry."

"What's it to him?"

"Population. He doesn't want their numbers to dwindle."

"Hmm." Spencer sipped his coffee again. "You could bring her down here. She'd be safe here."

"She has a sick mom. They have no one else. They're a package."

"Man, you sure know how to pick 'em. First time in love and you've got yourself a shit-storm brewing."

"I know it."

"What are you going to do?"

"I want to talk to Addy first. She's a medic and worst-case scenario, she can call her mom about Elena's mom. Elena said heart trouble, but they don't have a doctor up there."

"Okay. So, you want to see if they can help her mom?"

"I know they'll help her. And I'll cover any costs. But I want to make sure that moving her won't cause a heart attack. That would be a shit way to start out a relationship."

"Yeah, it would." Spencer scratched his chin. "Then what?"

"I want to talk to Emmy and Chase."

"You mean from RAPTOR?"

"Yeah. Chase is a doctor, but he's also a scientist. What if he could work with Elena and she could make a form of the elixir to help people. He could help her with it."

Spencer sat up straight. "That's actually a great idea, Aid."

"That's what I've lain awake all night thinking about."

"Where did you go with her?"

He took a deep breath. "The rental. It's still under

lease with us for another month. It was the only place I could think of where we could talk without being seen."

"So, answer this and know I don't care as long as you're safe. Was that Elena you snuck out of a container the other night?"

He swallowed. "Yes. It was after a security check, I saw her across the road watching for me. I didn't know where we could talk without being seen, so I opened the container and we stepped in there."

Spencer sipped his coffee. "Aid, how long have you two been seeing each other on the sly?"

"It started last fall the night of the Bourbon Ball."

Spencer whistled. "That's something. I had no idea."

"I guess that's good. It means we've been careful."

He laid his elbows on his thighs. His coffee cup was held in his left hand, the thumb on his right hand absently brushed the bracelet Elena had made him.

"If you're asking me, I think your plan is good, Aid. Speak with Addy. Then Emmy and Chase. But for god's sake, be careful. You are not well-liked up there and if they catch you with one of their women, they'll kill you, and that's not being melodramatic. Especially if they want her to marry and have babies. You're messing with an asset. The only one up there who brews their elixir. You're stepping into a big nasty pile of shit here."

"I know, Spence. It's all I've been thinking of."

"One last thing, then I'm going to eat Lara's cookies. If you are successful in bringing her down here, you won't be able to stay. They'll make life hell for you both. And us for good measure."

"I've thought that too. It helps that Myles will be here in a week. You won't be shorthanded. But I do know things will get dicey."

Spencer slapped him on the shoulder and strode back to the house.

Aidyn sighed and followed him to the house. Or, The HOG. He grinned, he liked it. HOG.

26

Her thoughts were all over the board. She wanted to march out there and kick over the still and tell Craig to shove his dick up his ass. It satisfied her to think of saying it. But, as she moved her jaw, and the pain shot to her ear, she wasn't sure she was ready for a beating. So, she put on her apron, kissed her mom on the cheek, and strode out the door.

She stared ahead as she neared the brew house, eager to get busy and let the words of this morning roll off her back. But she carried a new determination in her belly to leave this place. She could clean houses in town. At least, once she learned how to turn on showers and all the things she'd need to learn about living in an actual house. Aidyn had opened her eyes last night, to many things. One of them being, she loved him. That was the biggest one of all the things.

She knew it in her gut now. But she didn't know how he felt about her. She pushed back her feelings of inferiority. It didn't matter that she'd never seen a toilet—she wondered if he knew how to brew a healing elixir. No, she didn't know how to turn on the shower, but she'd bet he didn't know a mandrake from a chamomile flower.

She read books. Mostly things about plants and flowers, but she'd learned. She could read and write, and she could think.

But time was running out now. She built the fire under the still and began pouring in her emulsified plant extracts and water into the top. She set a clean bottle under the spigot, and she lined up her other bottles to transfer them out as needed today.

She filled pails with her emulsion and lined it up on the workbench so she could keep pouring. She wasn't in a hurry to get this brew done, she was in a hurry to steal a small sampling of it and take it down to Aidyn tonight. Maybe he could find use for it to help her survive in town. That was, if he wanted to help her and her mom. That was the other thing. She'd need to think about the safety of moving her mom.

From the corner of her eye she saw Craig watching her. She ignored him and kept herself busy. No doubt he'd station someone to watch her, too.

"Elena?"

She turned at Theresa's voice. "Oh, good morning, Theresa."

"I'm sorry. I didn't mean to startle you."

"It's alright. I was lost in my head. How can I help you?"

"What did you need help with today? I'll make your mama and you breakfast. But is there something you need to have done?"

"Yeah, Theresa, there is. While I'm out here today, I can begin planting seeds to start them for spring planting.

Do you mind bringing my supplies out here? Mama can tell you where everything is."

"Sure." Theresa smiled and skipped off. It was hard not to like her, but Elena planned on being wary. She'd keep her busy out here when she wasn't cooking so she didn't have time to sit with her mom or snoop. Just in case Craig asked her to look around.

She poured more emulsion into the still as she could hear the boiling and she saw Craig walk along the edge of the center circle and to the meeting area where he'd no doubt tell his council about this morning. Luckily all of them were married, so he'd get no volunteers there.

Theresa approached with a wooden crate filled with her jars and seeds. "Here you go."

"Thank you. Let's set it on the ground near the fire so the seeds don't cool off."

"Sure."

Theresa stood and brushed her hands together. "I'll be back with your jars."

"Thank you."

Elena checked the still, added wood, then knelt down to sort her seeds and supplies for planting. It also kept her out of Craig's eyeline, so that was a bonus and most of the reason she was doing this. Plus it gave her a smidgen of privacy to sort her items for later.

Theresa arrived with another wooden crate filled with glass jars and containers to start seeds.

"Here you go."

"Oh, thank you Theresa. I appreciate it."

"Do you need anything else?"

"After you make breakfast, if you'd like to come out and help me, I'd sure appreciate the help."

Theresa smiled ear to ear. "I'd love that. Thank you."

This time she actually skipped across the center circle. She was only fourteen. Craig would no doubt force her to marry soon too.

She checked the still and listened to the boil, but saw no condensation dripping yet, so she continued sorting her supplies.

She heard footsteps approach, and she knew it was Craig. Her stomach dropped and she took a deep breath to keep her temper in check, then waited for him to say something.

"Elena, what are you doing?"

"I'm sorting my seeds and getting them ready to start so they're ready to plant as soon as the ground warms."

"I've never seen you do this before."

"I've never had to brew this time of year before."

She refused to look at him.

"I'm sorry for the way things went this morning."

He was sorry? She finally lifted her head to look at him, but she said nothing.

"Look. This is all new for all of us. But we lost people in the brawl with the townies last fall. You know this. I'm simply worried."

"Forcing people to marry someone they don't love isn't going to achieve your goals, Craig. I'm sorry to be blunt. But I don't want to be tied to someone I don't love and I sure as hell don't want to bring children into a loveless home."

"I have another proposition for you to consider."

"A proposition?"

She stood but kept her seeds and supplies between them. She shoved her hands in her pockets.

"What if you had my child? Hanalore and I will raise it, since we can't seem to have our own. It would help me to do my part in the population increase and you wouldn't be burdened."

Her mouth literally hung open. "You want me to have a baby for you?"

"Yes. If you do this, I won't require you to marry."

"It's either or?"

"Yes."

She sucked in enough air to fill her lungs. Letting it out slowly she swallowed. "Then I suppose you'll want the recipe for the elixir since it would be my child and the heir to the recipe."

His jaw ground together but he said nothing other than, "I'll give you until tomorrow to give me an answer." Then he stomped across the clearing to the meeting hall.

27

Aidyn watched Addy process his information.

"So, weight gain, lethargic, slow heart rate. Anything else?"

"She didn't say. Just that the woman up there who is their doctor listened to her heart and said it was failing."

"Okay." Addy looked at the notes she'd made and pressed her lips together. "I'm not a diagnostician. Medic is far different than doctor."

"I'm aware. Will you discuss it with your mom?"

"Of course. I'll call her in a minute and see what she thinks. Is there any way I can see...What's her name?"

"Grace Dorsey."

"Okay. Grace. Is there any way I can see Grace to make a better determination?"

Aidyn sat back in his chair. "We're not very popular up there and bringing another medical professional may really set them off." He grinned. "So let's see if we can do it."

Addy grinned. "I'm all for it, but sure don't want to be the start of another war."

He leaned in and lowered his voice. "I'm meeting with Elena tonight. I'll see if we can sneak you up the mountain to do a better assessment of Grace's condition."

"Okay." She stood. "I'll go call my mom."

Aidyn stood as well. "Thanks, Addy."

She sauntered away and he went in search of Tate. His next difficult discussion. He stepped into the kitchen and found it empty. Cutting across the living room he knocked on the closed office door.

"Come in."

He slid the barn-style door open to see Tate sitting at his desk. "You have a minute?"

"Of course."

Aidyn entered the office and sat on one of the leather chairs facing him.

"What's up?"

Taking a deep breath, he leaned forward. "I have feelings for Elena. We've been meeting in private for a few months now."

Tate kept his face neutral and sat back in his chair. "Okay."

Aidyn continued. "She wants to leave the mountain and I want to help her. She's the brewer up there. It'll be contentious, but with Craig as the president, things are changing for the worse and time is running out for Elena."

"Running out. In what way?"

"Craig asked her to make another batch of elixir to pay the taxes, which she's doing right now. But he's also told her she has to marry and have kids to help keep their population up."

"Holy fuck!"

"Right. Add to that a sick mom and all I see is a battle coming to remove them from the mountain."

"How sick is the mom?"

"I don't know. They think a heart condition but there's no confirmation of that from a medical professional. I've asked Addy for help and she's speaking with her mom right now. But it seems as though she will need assistance coming down. Once the extraction is started, there'll be no turning back. Elena would suffer the consequences of aborting an extraction. Her mom as well. I can't let that happen."

"Are you in love with her?"

He took another deep breath and let the calm settle over him.

"Yes." It was the first time he'd actually admitted it out loud and it wasn't hard. Scary—sure. He hoped he wasn't making a mistake here. They would be disrupting many lives, including his teammates.

"We can't go in without a plan. We have to prepare and know the area. Can you ask Elena to draw a map or show us where everyone is situated? We have some knowledge, but not enough to go up there and take two of their people. And that's what it will look like—a kidnapping. It could start a tit-for-tat scenario."

"I'm aware and I'm sorry. I don't know what else to do."

"Is she in danger now?"

"She doesn't think so. Other than Craig making noise about getting married. But she's brewing their second batch now and she thinks, until the batch is finished, she's safe."

"When is the batch finished?"

"A week."

"Okay. See if you can get a map from Elena and we'll go from there."

He stood to leave but halted. "Thanks, Tate. I'm sorry

and sure don't mean to create a mess up there or down here. But I want to be with her and she wants to leave the mountain."

Tate nodded. "I only want to ask one question. She's not using you to get her out of there is she? In other words, once we stir up this hornet's nest, we're the ones who will suffer the consequences. Is she sticking around, or will she take off for parts unknown and leave us with the shit?"

He swallowed. "I've asked myself that question a thousand times. I believe she's legit. She has feelings for me, too." He shrugged. "I don't know. It could be a bit of both. But I can't leave her up there. I won't have a moment of peace knowing I left a woman up there to be treated as if she has no rights. To be forced to marry and birth children with someone she doesn't love. But we haven't gotten down to the nitty gritty of things."

"You need to get gritty, Aid. Soon."

He swallowed what felt like a hot rock in his throat. Hearing that out loud hurt. He'd been thinking it but pushed it aside and told himself to stop being a baby. The final conclusion he'd come to around five this morning was that even if she was using him to get herself and her mom off the mountain, it would be worth it. Living up there being someone's baby-maker without love was no way to live. So, he'd nurse his broken heart and revel in the fact that he'd helped her start a new and better life. That would have to give him solace in the long dark nights when he felt low.

He strode back to his bedroom and pulled his phone from his pocket. For the fourth time today, he'd have to tell his story and then he'd have to tell it again when he called his parents because they should know what's going on and it should be from him. Not reading the GHOST reports of the extraction.

He pulled up his contacts and tapped Emersyn's name. His heartbeat increased as he listened for the phone to connect. He hoped Emmy and Chase would be able to help Elena and he knew they'd have to move back to Indiana once she was free. Craig would make her the poster child for bad behavior and traitorism and she'd never be safe here.

28

Elena moved through the motions after speaking with Craig. She was faced with two impossible options. Not physically impossible, but in her mind, neither was an option she wanted to choose.

As the condensation began to drip, she set a small jar under the spigot to collect the liquid which was the same as gold up here. As soon as the small bottle had filled to about half, she replaced it with a larger bottle and set the small bottle in one of the wooden crates with her seeds in it. Hiding it behind the material tucked around the edge of the basket.

She then set out her bundles of seeds, filled her containers partially with soil, then planted her seeds. She used small sticks she'd cut down and flattened to label the seed containers. Theresa came out to help her and she tasked her with filling the containers with soil and flattening sticks to write on.

They largely worked in silence and Elena was grateful for it. She wasn't in the mood to make polite conversation.

"Elena? Is it alright if I go make lunch for our mamas?"

She nodded. "Of course. I didn't realize it had gotten so late."

"You seem rather preoccupied."

Elena nodded but said nothing and Theresa ambled to her own cabin instead of going to Elena's.

She replaced the filled bottle under the spigot, corked it closed, then lifted the jar to the workbench to label it with the date.

"Elena?"

She turned to see Kent standing at the edge of the brewing area. "Hi, Kent. How can I help you?"

He turned to see if anyone was listening then faced her. "I heard Craig wants you to marry. I wanted to let you know that I'll marry you. I know it's not a love match, but to be honest, there's no one up here for me either. We might be able to make a decent life you and me."

She stared at Kent. Someone she'd known, all of his life. Blue eyes and dark hair and not as harsh or crude as most of them up here. And to be honest, he had an education and wanted to make life up here better for their people. She could do worse.

But.

He wasn't Aidyn.

She tucked a loose lock of hair behind her ear. Her fingers shook slightly as she gathered her thoughts. His eyes watched her fingers then slid back to her eyes. "Look, I know this is coming from left field, but I'm trying to help."

She locked her hands together in front of her to keep her fingers still and swallowed. "Thank you for the offer. May I think about it?"

He nodded. "Sure."

He stepped back two steps, then bobbed his head and turned toward his cabin.

Her belly flipped and she swallowed to keep from vomiting. Inhaling long steady breaths and letting them out slowly seemed to ease the discomfort. But the dread that settled over her shoulders seemed much too heavy to bear.

She leaned against the workbench and stared at the seeds until they blurred. She sniffed and pulled a handkerchief from her apron pocket and dabbed at her nose. Tucking it back in its pocket, she took an unsteady breath and let it out. She turned to check the bottle under the spigot, pulled an empty bottle from the shelf, and replaced the full one. She added more water and emulsified herbs and stoked the fire.

Could she live like this for the rest of her life? What she was about to ask Aidyn to do would cause so much trouble. She didn't think Kent would ever beat her. Maybe after they had one or two babies, he'd not even want to have sex with her anymore.

That thought caused her stomach to turn and this time the breakfast she'd eaten spilled out. She ran to the back side of the brewing area and emptied her stomach. Her knees shook and her body felt damp with sweat. She righted herself and shuffled to the cup of water she had on the workbench. Swishing water in her mouth and spitting it out, she took a tentative sip from the water and let it slide down her throat.

"Here you go." Theresa's voice broke her haze. "Oh, Elena, are you alright? You're pale as a sheet."

"I'm fine, Theresa. I'm okay."

"Are you sure, I can ask Mama to come out here."

She held up her hand and shook her head. "No. Please. I'm fine."

"I brought you some lunch. Maybe that will make you feel better."

She swallowed and nodded. "Yes. That will probably help very much. Thank you."

Theresa stepped back. "If you change your mind, let me know and I'll have Mama come and look at you. In the meantime, I'm taking your mama some lunch and I'll be back in a while to finish helping you."

"Thank you."

Theresa stepped away and she crept to the plate of food and lifted the cover. Theresa's biscuits were dripping honey and looked delicious. Smoked venison and a dot of caramelized sugar as a sweet. Her heart felt like lead for thinking badly of Theresa when she made such nice meals for them. She simply didn't trust anyone up here these days and most of the folks were on edge because Craig was a completely different man than his father had ever been. It caused everyone to distrust each other.

With shaking fingers she picked up a biscuit and took a small bite. It was good. The bread helped her stomach somewhat, but she'd eat it slowly in case she had any more instances of her stomach rebelling. She'd do well to keep her thoughts clear of all that made her sick. Focus on Aidyn and their night together last night.

His face came to view in her mind, and she closed her eyes a moment to see him clearly. He smiled in her mind, and she stared at his beautiful face. His gentle hands brushed her cheeks before his soft lips touched hers and she put her fingers to her lips as she remembered how he felt.

"You're lost in thought."

Her eyes flew open to see Craig staring at her.

"What?"

"You looked lost in thought."

"Yeah."

As she waited for him to say something else, she nibbled on her biscuit again and he eventually walked away. He'd be around all the time while she was pregnant if she had a baby for him. It would be sickening. Not to mention having sex with him to get pregnant. And, what if it didn't work the first time. Her stomach rolled again, and she turned and sucked in a huge breath.

His mom sighed heavily and he couldn't tell if it was a good swoon-sigh or if she was frustrated. He waited for her to say something but all that met his ears was silence.

His dad finally broke the silence. "Aid, we love you. We always have. And, we'll support you in anything you want to do. But please make sure this is something you want. You'll be creating a shitstorm for two towns."

"I know, Dad. I've thought about this a lot. I can't leave her up there to be reduced to a dog having litters for a man or men who only want to increase the population. And what kind of a life is that for the kids? They're being created to be a number. To probably die for a cause they had nothing to do with. This is the shit you've been fighting your whole lives, my whole life, and what I was trained to do from the time I was five."

His mom spoke. "You're right, Aidyn. You're right." She took a deep breath. "We just want you to be sure. And then we want you to be careful. Do it carefully. And, with your teammates. Not on your own."

"Mom, I'll work with Tate and we'll set out a plan and we'll execute the plan like we're supposed to."

His dad replied, "We're proud of you, Aidyn. I know your heart's invested in this, but you're doing what's right even though it's hard and will stir up so much more trouble."

"Thanks, Dad."

"Keep us posted on what's happening."

"I will. Love you both."

He ended his call, heaved out a breath to release the heaviness sitting on his chest and left his bedroom to see what Tate had going on. Technically this was their day off, but they didn't really have days off. They'd agreed on twelve-hour shifts so they could rest. That was only if there wasn't shit going on. He wished Myles was here already; they could use the extra set of hands.

He peered in the office and found it empty. He walked out to the kitchen and found it empty as well. Hearing laughter outside, he strode through the garage and to the backyard where his friends were playing catch. Just like a normal day. But it sure didn't feel normal to him.

Spencer waved him over. He gave Maya a wide birth as he strode past her, and she cackled. She was notorious for tackling them all. As he neared Spencer, he caught the ball Henry threw him, then waved him off.

"Tate went in to talk to the sheriff."

"Why?"

"He wants him to be on alert in case they retaliate by coming down here and try to kidnap someone."

"Yeah." He heaved out a breath. "I'm so sorry it's coming to this. But we don't have a choice."

"You don't. We all know that. And, in some ways, it might be good. We'll really find out how organized they are and if they come down here, we can lock them up. It might start something good here, Aidyn."

"Right." He glanced at the mountain and hoped things were going alright for Elena up there. He hated that he couldn't be there to protect her.

———

Aidyn parked his truck in the lot across from the big tree. He was in the shadow of the building, but he had a perfect view of the area around the base of the tree.

He was slightly early but wanted to be here in case Elena managed to come down earlier than usual. He'd spent the entire day thinking of all possible scenarios to get her and her mom off the mountain without bloodshed and war. He felt stupid that he hadn't come up with anything.

All their dealings with the BRR to date had shown them that the BRR was willing to enact violence with the slightest provocation. What they were about to do wasn't slight at all.

After an hour, he became restless. After two hours he was worried. He didn't know where her cabin was, or he'd go right up there and get her now.

He stepped from his truck and paced around it, burning off some of his worry and energy. Finally, he saw the vines move and he froze.

She rose from the vines and hurried across the road toward him. Once her feet hit the parking lot she picked up speed and he ran to meet her. She jumped in his arms and he scooped her up effortlessly and hurried them to the relative safety of his truck. Opening the door he set her on the ground and pressed his lips to hers. He heard her gasp.

He pulled back to look into her eyes with the light from inside his truck. The left side of her face was bruised and swollen.

"Who hit you?"

Tears filled her eyes and he softened his voice. He ushered her into his truck and closed the door. Stomping around the back of his truck, he sucked in big breaths of air to calm himself. After climbing into the driver's seat, he turned to Elena and examined her face.

"Honey. Who hit you?"

Her bottom lip trembled. "Craig."

"Why?"

"I snipped at him this morning. He told me it was my duty to marry and have babies and I asked him why he and Hanalore didn't have babies if it was so important." She swallowed. "He slapped me. I think harder than he meant to. He apologized later."

He held the steering wheel with an iron grip and his jaw clenched tightly.

He took a deep breath. "I'm sorry this happened."

Tears fell down her cheeks and he swiped them gently away, careful not to press on her swollen cheek. Leaning over, he opened his glove box and pulled a tissue from a box he had in there.

He handed it to her and she stared at it. His brows wrinkled and he cocked his head.

"It's a tissue. To wipe your tears."

"Tissue."

She gently took it from his fingers and rubbed it between hers. She dabbed at her tears and looked at the tissue.

"It's falling apart."

"It's disposable. Once you use it, you throw it away."

"Why? You could use a handkerchief."

Nodding, he said, "Yeah. We used to. But people down here got too busy to have to wash them. Plus this is more sanitary."

"Okay."

He started his truck and turned onto the road leading to the HOG. He needed his teammates to see she was in danger. They didn't question his decision. Not vocally. But he knew what he was asking made them all uneasy.

"Where are we going?"

"To the HOG. Our home. My teammates and mine. Tate wants you to draw a map of the mountain and where your cabin is."

"Okay."

She was quiet for a long time. Then she softly asked, "Are they mad?"

"Oh Elena. They trust me and I trust you. You have nothing to worry about." Aidyn murmured soothingly.

30

Aidyn held her hand as he drove. She needed the connection. His hands were strong but always gentle with her.

He stopped at a gate and rolled his window down with just a button. The old trucks they had up on the mountain had handles you turned to roll the windows down.

He waved a card in front of a black box and the gate opened. It slid to one side, and he drove through it. She turned as they neared a building and saw the gate close behind them.

He drove around the brick building and at the back were a bunch of big metal doors. He pushed a button on his truck roof and a door opened. He drove into the building.

She held her breath until he stopped the truck, and he squeezed her hand.

"Welcome to The HOG."

"Why do you call it a pig?"

He chuckled then kissed her fingers. "It's not a pig, it's HOG. Home. Office. Garage."

"Oh."

He chuckled and jumped from his truck. She watched him walk around to her side. She looked for the door handle and just as she found it, he opened the door for her.

He smiled at her. It was the beautiful smile she'd recalled in her mind all day when she needed to calm herself.

"Are you ready?"

She felt her lips tremble and she couldn't say anything so she nodded. He'd be with her so she would be safe. It wasn't like up on the mountain.

He reached in and lifted her down, then he pulled her close and held her tightly to his body. She wrapped her arms around his waist and squeezed him tightly to her. She felt the tears flood her eyes and her nose tingled.

"Hey, you're shaking. It'll be alright."

She only nodded. His big strong hands smoothed up and down her back and she stilled to feel it. She prayed she'd absorb some of his strength and confidence.

After a few moments, he pulled away. "They're waiting for us, baby."

She nodded again and he reached into the truck and pulled out another tissue. He handed it to her and she opened her hand where the other one lay crumpled up. He took it from her hand and grinned.

"Are you ready?"

She nodded and let him lead her to a door. He opened it and let her step into a huge kitchen. Much nicer than the one last night. This one was bigger than her whole cabin. Probably two of her cabins. They had cupboards with doors on them all along the wall and she stared at it all. The stove and refrigerator looked like metal.

Aidyn stepped in and pulled a handle on a door under a big counter in the middle of the room and tossed her tissue in there. She craned her neck to see it.

"It's garbage."

"In your cabinets?"

He chuckled. "In this one."

He closed the door and took her hand. They sauntered through the big kitchen, and he pointed to the right to a huge wooden table. "That's the dining room."

She swallowed and they continued through a room with three big leather sofas and glass tables and pretty lights. The floor was hardwood, and it was perfect. Her head bobbed around as she looked at the room. It was stunning.

Aidyn brought them to another room, much smaller than the other rooms they'd gone through and a man sat at a table with papers on it.

He stood when they entered, and he smiled and held his hand out to her.

"Do you remember Tate?" She laid her hand in Tate's and he squeezed gently and bobbed her hand up and down.

"It's nice to meet you, Elena." Her cheeks burned under his scrutiny.

She whispered. "It's nice to meet you too."

Tate's eyes shifted to Aidyn's, then he sat. Aidyn motioned to a chair behind her and she sat. He took the chair next to her.

Tate pulled some paper from a machine behind his desk then said, "Why don't we go into the dining room where it'll be comfortable."

Aidyn stood. "That's a great idea."

He took her hand, and they strode through the big

rooms again and her mind reeled at how they lived. It was amazing and it made her feel insignificant and less than. She'd never had a place like this.

They stopped at the huge table and Tate dropped the papers at the end, then turned toward the kitchen and stepped away.

Aidyn pulled the chair nearest Tate out and smiled at her. "Sit here, Elena. Tate will want to see the maps with you."

"Where will you be?"

Her heart began racing and she swallowed a lump in her throat.

"I'll be right here." He patted the chair next to hers.

She sat stiffly in the chair, her hands in her lap.

Tate came back with a plate of cookies and cups of coffee. He left then came back with little packets in a bowl. "I don't know if you like cream or sugar, both are here."

He sat and she stared at the bowl with the little square packets. She turned her head and caught Aidyn's gaze. He grinned at her then kissed her temple.

He picked up a white packet. "This is creamer." He pointed to the word creamer and she smiled. He pulled another packet that was tan in color. "This is sugar."

She nodded but made no move to do anything because she wasn't sure what she was supposed to do. Aidyn ripped open a packet of creamer and she immediately remembered him opening a condom last night and her cheeks heated. She felt her neck warm too.

Aidyn poured the powder into his cup, and she furrowed her brows. "I thought that was cream."

"Creamer, hon. It's powdered cream. Cow's cream."

She nodded. "Okay." She fidgeted.

Aidyn touched her shoulder. "Do you have coffee up there?"

She shook her head. "I only have tea and water."

Tate stood, "I think we have tea here."

"No." She stopped because that came out louder than she intended. "It's okay. I'll try coffee."

Tate sat again and she picked up her cup. She inhaled the aroma. She didn't have anything to compare it to, but it smelled good, and she closed her eyes.

She sipped gently at the hot liquid and scrunched her face. "That's bitter."

Aidyn and Tate laughed. "It can be."

Aidyn handed her a packet of the creamer. "That's why I use this."

She tore the packet open and poured the contents into her coffee and watched as it disappeared. Her coffee turned a pretty tan color and she grinned. She picked up her coffee again and sipped.

"Mmm, that's better."

They both chuckled. Aidyn pointed to her jacket. "Do you want to take your jacket off?"

"Not yet."

"I thought I heard voices out here."

Lara walked into the room looking beautiful and confident and like she belonged here. Of course she belonged. Lara stopped near her chair and held her hand out.

Elena lay her hand in Lara's and they shook. This time she squeezed a little bit too and Lara smiled.

"It's nice to meet you, Elena. I'm Lara."

She nodded. "I know. You're famous up there."

Lara faltered on her way to sit on the other side of Tate. "Famous?"

"Everyone knows you're Kent's sister."

Lara swallowed but said nothing and Elena was immediately sorry she said anything.

Lara leaned in then. "What happened to you Elena? Oh my God, is your face... Did someone hit you?"

Elena held her hand over the left side of her face and looked down at her lap.

Lara came over to her chair once again and kneeled down in front of her. She spun the chair so she faced Lara. "You don't need to be embarrassed. I'm sorry I blurted it out like I did. I couldn't see the bruising before. Do you need an ice pack? I have one."

Before Elena could answer, Lara jumped up and strode to the refrigerator.

Elena's breathing faltered and she wanted to leave. She stood and turned to Aidyn. "I should go. I'm causing trouble. I don't mean to be trouble."

Aidyn stood and stepped up to her. He wrapped her in his arms and rested his cheek on the top of her head. His voice was soft as he crooned, "You're no trouble. You need assistance and we all want to help you."

Lara came to her side. She held her hand out and pulled a towel open. "This is an ice pack. It will help reduce the swelling. The towel over it is to buffer your skin from the cold. Hold it against your cheek."

She swallowed and held the ice against her cheek. It did feel better.

She sat again and tried to get her breathing under control.

Tate turned the papers on the table to her.

"Elena, these are maps of Hickory Hills. Can you show me on these maps where your house is?"

31

Aidyn watched with a proud heart as Elena pointed out places on the map at Tate's request. After she pointed out where she brewed the elixir she asked, "Why do you need to know this?"

Aidyn turned her chair toward him. She lowered the ice pack and stared into his eyes. Hers were clear and alert despite the day she'd had brewing all day.

"Elena, we want to help you get down here for good."

Her eyes filled with instant tears. "It's dangerous."

"Yes." His fingers brushed her bruised cheek. "It's dangerous for you as well."

She stared into his eyes but said nothing. "Can you tell me what happened today?"

She swallowed and took a deep breath. "I told you I sassed at Craig."

"Yes. You asked him why he didn't have children if he wanted the population to grow."

She nodded. "Yes."

"But what else happened today?"

"He...Craig. He came out to the brew shed and told me he was sorry. He offered me a concession."

"A concession?"

"Yes. He said if I would have his baby he wouldn't make me marry."

He sucked in a breath. "He what?"

"He gave me until tomorrow to give him an answer."

"No!" He stood and paced to the wall then came back to the table. His stomach twisted into a tight ball and threatened to bring up his dinner.

He sat next to her again, his breathing came in spurts and he tried to calm himself.

Elena reached for his hand. "I didn't say yes."

"What did you say?"

"He said I could think about it, and I didn't say anything else."

She laid the ice pack on the table with shaking fingers. He took her hands in his and squeezed. "You can't go back up there."

"I have to. My mom needs me. They'll punish her and let her die."

"Elena...You can't. It's not safe." He swallowed several times to rein in his emotions. "What will you say tomorrow when he demands an answer?"

She looked down at their clasped hands. "Kent said he'd marry me. He doesn't love me and I don't love him but I thought I'd tell Craig I'll marry Kent. It will buy me some time."

Lara sat back in her seat and Elena turned to her.

Lara leaned forward. "Kent offered to marry you?"

"He said there wasn't anyone else up there he wanted to marry and heard Craig was making trouble for me. He said we could maybe have a decent life."

The thought of her marrying anyone else slammed into Aidyn's gut like a sledgehammer. He struggled to get breath in his lungs.

Elena turned to him and took his hands in hers. "I'm not going to. Just buying time."

"Why. Why do you need time?"

"I need to figure out how to get Mom down the mountain."

Tate leaned forward. "That's what we're trying to figure out too, Elena. Adelaide, one of our teammates, is a medic. Her mother is a doctor. Aidyn shared your mom's symptoms with Addy today and she wants to see your mom. We want to sneak her up the mountain and into your cabin so she can assess your mom's condition."

Elena stared at Tate for a long time. "It's dangerous."

"We know."

"Why would you put yourself in danger for me?"

Tate's eyes landed on his. "Because we love Aidyn, and he loves you."

He closed his eyes. He hadn't told her he loved her yet. She turned to face him.

"Is that true?"

"Yes."

"You love me?"

"Yes. I love you."

She looked deeply into his eyes. "I love you too. I'm sorry I didn't tell you last night."

He leaned in and kissed her lips, careful not to hurt her face.

He pulled back slightly, "So, I spent the day talking to my teammates about you and your mom. I've told them all I love you and want to bring you down here. I called my parents and told them. And we've been trying to devise a plan to get you both safely down the mountain."

She reached into her jacket pocket. "I took this today. This is fresh brew and not cut. I was going to give it to you to see if you could use it for anything. It's powerful full strength. I usually use tea to cut it. It helps with breathing problems and some heart problems. But not my mom's."

She slid the small bottle onto the table and they all stared at it. "It will also make you high if not used properly, and it will give you stomach issues if you use too much."

Lara nodded. "My mom was hooked on it."

"Yes." She locked eyes with Lara. "I'm sorry. I didn't mean for anyone to get sick from it."

Lara leaned across the table and stretched her hand across. Elena laid her hand in Lara's and Lara smiled. "I know you didn't, and I don't hold you responsible. I hold my parents responsible for their actions."

Tate stood. "I'll call Addy. We need to go up tonight."

Aidyn rubbed her back. "Elena, we'll need you to lead us up there. Show us how you get around."

"It's risky. They are watching me now. It's why I was late."

"Can you find another way? Maybe on a different side of the mountain than the one you usually go?"

She swallowed and he stared into her eyes. She swallowed. "Yes. If you can drive us around the other side of the mountain, between here and Brookswood."

"I can do that."

"It will come up the south side of the mountain and where most of us don't go. There's a lot of brush and it's steep."

"We can manage it."

He watched her breath deeply a few times. "Okay. We don't have much time. The sun will be up in four hours."

They stood and he took her hand. Tate and Lara stepped away from the table and he softly apologized. "I'm sorry I didn't tell you last night how I felt. I guess I wasn't sure. Or it didn't occur to me or something. As soon as I started to tell Spencer about you, I knew."

Her lips turned up into a pretty smile. "It's okay. I didn't tell you, either. I was mad at myself all day that if I never got the chance to see you again, you'd never know that I loved you."

He pulled her to his chest and held her close. "You'll see me every day."

Aidyn pulled his truck to a stop at the base of the mountain in the parking lot of a closed-down bar. She saw headlights behind them and resisted the urge to turn and watch Tate park near them. Adelaide and Spencer were back there as well. She'd met them all tonight and was still speechless that they would risk harm to help her and her mom.

She turned and stared at Aidyn's profile. She loved him. She thanked God for bringing him into her life. Her heart fluttered thinking about him. Being with him. "Thank you."

He grinned, then leaned in and kissed her. "You're welcome. Thank you for coming into my life."

She chuckled. "I was just thinking the same thing. I'll remember to thank God for you every night."

"I will too."

He opened a small box. "Put this in your ear." He turned his head and pointed to his ear. "Like this."

She put the small bud into her ear. He then pulled a small black object from the box and pushed something on it. A green light flickered then turned off. "Clip this on your clothing where it's out of sight. It's the receiver to allow the earpiece to work."

He clicked his black box on. "So you can hear all of us in your ear."

She jumped when he spoke to her. She could hear him in her ear. As in, from the little thing in her ear.

"Tate on."

She jumped again. He chuckled. "We'll all have these on. We can hear each other. But, we only talk when something needs to be said. No chatting. Others close by may be able to hear us."

"Okay."

He kissed her lips, then held his finger to his lips and winked. She smiled and that wink made butterflies soar in her belly.

He left the truck and walked around to her door and opened it. He lifted her and set her feet gently on the ground. Tate and Adelaide joined them. Spencer came up behind them.

Aidyn softly spoke. "Elena, we'll be behind you since you know the way. If you hear something or someone just whisper, 'stop.'"

"Okay."

He looked at his teammates, "Mic checks."

Tate started. "Tate on."

"Adelaide on."

"Spencer on."

"Aidyn on."

She looked into his eyes and he nodded. "Oh, Elena on."

They nodded and Aidyn turned her toward the mountain. "Right behind you."

She swallowed and neared the base of the mountain. They seldom used this side of the mountain, though just recently a couple of the guys had been coming down and making deals with people for the elixir. Hopefully they weren't out and about this late at night. Or, actually, early in the morning.

She moved into the brush, slowly moving forward, feeling her way with the toe of her shoes for rocks or downed branches. They moved quietly, though Aidyn and his teammates made more noise than she did. That was something she could do that they couldn't. Her confidence grew a bit and she focused on her task.

The real trick would be getting them into the cabin without being seen. But she had an idea for that.

The terrain grew steeper, and her breathing labored slightly. She could hear Aidyn's breathing as they climbed, which was a comfort.

They landed on a plateau, and she stopped to rest, allowing the others to do the same. "It's one more mile up."

They nodded as they let their breathing settle. When she recognized their even breathing, she started up again. She found a used path, likely from the guys who were trading in Brookswood, and she used it to help the others climb.

She listened carefully, turning her head back and forth. Even the animals slept at this time of day.

Finally nearing their homestead on the mountain, she slowed and turned to them and whispered, "I need to move ahead alone in case Craig has someone watching. When I know it's clear I'll let you know. You'll need to follow my path."

Aidyn nodded. "Roger."

She stopped and furrowed her brows. "We don't have a Roger."

"Sorry. I mean alright."

Nodding, she crept slowly along the path to the very edge of their camp. She peered around the back of her cabin, and the shrubs alongside of it. The woodpile was at the back, so she picked up an armful of wood, should anyone see her and question her. She crept quietly along the side of the cabin and opened the door.

"Come quickly," she whispered.

Aidyn, Adelaide, Spencer, and Tate hustled along the edge of the cabin and she held the door for them to enter.

Once inside, she felt ridiculous as they filled the space entirely and she barely had room to move past them.

"Maybe if three of you sat at the table, there'd be more room."

Aidyn, Tate, and Spencer pulled chairs out quietly and she motioned for Adelaide to come to the back with her.

She held her finger to her lips when her mom sat up.

"Don't talk, Mama."

She sat at the edge of her mom's bed and gathered their hands together. "This is Adelaide. She's a medic with Aidyn and his team. She wants to examine you and see if she can tell what's wrong with you. Please let her examine you."

"Elena, we'll get in so much trouble if anyone finds out."

"Then be quiet and let Adelaide examine you so they can leave."

She squeezed her mom's hands to reassure her, then moved over to sit on the edge of her bed as Adelaide moved next to her mom.

She listened to Adelaide's soft voice and intelligent

questions, and she felt so much relief that someone with some education about medicine would be helping to figure out what was wrong with her mom.

Aidyn was watching her and she felt nervous. Most of that nervousness was the danger they were in just being here, but after seeing where and how they all lived, she didn't compare. She couldn't compare. What did he see in her anyway? She was simple compared to them.

She realized though that they were likely thirsty after climbing up the mountain and she should be a better hostess. She neared the table where they sat quietly. "May I get you a cup of water?"

Aidyn smiled at her but shook his head. "I'm alright. Thank you."

Spencer and Tate both shook their heads and she was now filled with doubt. What should she be doing? The fire had died down, so she skirted around the table and added a couple logs to the fire, poked it with the poker to settle the logs on the hot coals then stood and brushed her hands together. When she turned, they were all watching her and her face burned.

Aidyn motioned with his hand for her to come closer. Swallowing she obeyed.

"How often do you have to stoke the fire?"

"Every few hours. This time of year. The cabin is pretty cozy so it stays warm enough."

"It's very nice. Did you build it?"

She chuckled. "No, my daddy built it. I carried the stones for the fireplace though. That was my job. At the time I was only about twelve. He died the following year. It's just Mama and me now."

Aidyn's lips turned down slightly. "I'm sorry for the loss of your father."

She smiled thinking of her dad. "He was bigger than life. I thought he was the best builder and hunter around. He took such good care of Mama and me. Back then, Mama was the brewer up here."

"I can tell he built this cabin with love."

She cocked her head. "How so?"

Aidyn pointed to the mantle, a peeled half log. Her father had carved little scroll details on it. "He carved on the mantle. Precise and detailed. There are hooks at both ends for you to hang items and every stone is neatly placed. Even Everett didn't have that detail in his cabin."

She stared at him for a long time. He noticed little things.

Adelaide ambled to the table. "She's fine. I don't think it's her heart at all. Her heartbeat is strong and steady. I think it's hypothyroidism. Once she's on medication, she'll feel so much better."

Elena's hand flew to her mouth and she sucked in air. "Really?"

Adelaide smiled the most beautiful smile. "Really. I'm going to tell my mom what I found, but I'd bet she'll agree with me. Once we get Grace down the mountain, we'll have her see the doctor and confirm the diagnosis."

33

Aidyn glanced at Grace, who still sat on the edge of her bed, wringing her hands together.

"Now we just need to figure out how to get her down the mountain."

Elena moved to the back of the cabin and he and his teammates chatted about how to get Grace down the mountain.

He asked Addy, "Can she walk?"

"She says yes, but she's slow. Her energy levels are low, she tires. The only thing I can think of is we'll need to take turns helping her down."

Tate shook his head. "It'll take too long the way we came up."

Spencer nodded. "I agree. What if one of us goes down the mountain and drives a truck around to the side nearest Glen Hollow. If we take her down that way, we can drive partially up the mountain and get Grace into the truck from there."

"They'll hear that for certain."

Elena came back to the table. "I have a plan. I'll tell

Craig I'll have a baby for him if he lets Mama go down to get help."

"No." His stomach knotted and he felt like vomiting. After punching something that is.

"I'm not going to do it Aidyn. Just buy some time."

"He won't let you out of his sight if that's the case."

"I'll tell him I have to take her down myself."

"And what if he escorts you down there?"

"I'll have to deal with that. But he hates it down there so I can't see him going down the mountain."

"But, if he does. What then? Or what if he tells you he has to sleep with you first then he'll let you take your mom down there?"

She opened her mouth but closed it.

He watched the emotions flit across her face. Her shoulders sank and she lay a hand across her tummy. It occurred to him then, when they'd had sex in the shower, they didn't use protection. What if she was pregnant with his child right now? The thought scared and excited him.

"No, Elena. We can't risk it. He's unpredictable and he's not stupid."

"I've given him no reason to think I'd leave and stay down there."

"By asking for a doctor from town to look at your mom, you're essentially saying you don't trust the doctor you have up here."

"She's not a real doctor. She's a medicine woman at best."

"What have others done when they've been sick?"

Her eyes watered as she stared at the fireplace and his heart dropped. "They died." She sniffed. "My dad, died."

He moved to her, like a magnet connecting without resistance. He wrapped his arms around her and held her close. Over her head he saw Grace watching them. Grace smiled softly and nodded.

She stood and waited a moment to gain her balance then ambled toward them. He loosened his hold on Elena and she turned toward her mom.

Grace laid her hand on Adelaide's shoulder and squeezed.

"Why don't you all go back down and I'll get myself down the hill this morning."

"Mama, you can't do that."

Grace nodded. "I can." She took a deep breath. "I was not doing much and being very careful because I was afraid my heart would give out and you'd be left all alone, Elena."

Grace smiled at him. "You're not alone now and Adelaide tells me my heart is strong and steady. So, I'll go out with your basket to gather herbs today and I'll slip down there by myself."

"Mama, you'll have to do that early. When I don't show up this morning to brew, Craig is going to raise holy hell."

"Yes. He will. But I'll already be down there. If someone is able to pick me up, I won't be in danger."

Elena stepped to her mom and hugged her. Grace wrapped her arms around her daughter's waist and he felt like things were going to be alright.

Elena turned to him. "Are you alright with all of this? We'll lean on you a lot, Aidyn, and if you change your mind and want to walk away, this would be the time to do it."

He shook his head. "I'm not changing my mind. I love you, Elena."

Her cheeks tinted a pretty pink and she ducked her head slightly. "I love you too. But..." She motioned between herself and her mom. "We're a lot. You saw all the things I don't know about your world. Mama was born up here too. She's ignorant, just like me."

"You're not ignorant, Elena. Neither of you. You haven't seen some of the things we have day to day, but I haven't seen what you do day to day."

Grace nudged Elena. "Go on now. Go. I'll be down there in about an hour. I'll leave right behind you."

Elena pulled some little pouches from glass jars and tucked them in the pockets of her leather apron. She stared at the fireplace for a few moments and Aidyn took his phone out and snapped a picture of the fireplace.

"What did you do?" She asked.

"I took a picture for you." He tapped his phone and pulled up his photos and showed her. She stared at it for a long time then turned his phone to show her mom.

"Well, isn't that something?" Grace whispered.

Elena handed him his phone and he saw the unshed tears in her eyes. "Thank you."

He kissed her forehead and snapped pictures of her entire cabin. Someday they'd look back at these and remember this day. And Elena would remember her early days.

"Ready?"

"Yes." She gasped. "No, wait." She hurried to the chest at the end of her bed and pulled her gloves from inside. She put them on and smiled as she brushed the leather against her cheeks. Her eyes landed on his. "I had to keep them hidden so no one would know."

He nodded, but his lips formed a straight line. What was it like to live each day afraid of doing the smallest thing for fear of reprisal?

"Honey, we've got to go." Grace reminded her.

Elena nodded, hugged her mom once again and walked to the door.

He stepped toward Grace as the others lined up to leave. "Are you sure you'll be alright? We can have one of us waiting for you halfway down to assist you."

"You're a very nice man. I see why Elena loves you. But I feel fine. I'll be tired but I'm excited to be able to get out and do something on my own."

Elena pulled a cloth from the counter and laid it on the table. She pulled a pencil she had hidden from the fireplace mantle. "Mama, I'm leaving a note for Kent. He should have the cabin. He was willing to help me."

"You're a sweet young woman, Elena."

She wrote, "Kent, the cabin is yours."

She pocketed the pencil, then crossed to the door and lifted the lock. She looked back at them. "Let me make sure no one is out and about. If they are, I'll go around back and grab firewood. If not, I'll let you know."

He grinned at her. "Whisper." Then tapped his ear.

34

Elena stepped outside and stood on the stoop. No one seemed to be about yet and the sun had an hour or so before it rose. She scurried around the side of the cabin and whispered. "Clear."

At the back of her cabin, she waited until she saw Adelaide behind her, then she continued to the path they'd brought up here. The sky was at its darkest now, but the path was relatively clear. The only protrusions were rocks jutting out of the dirt here and there.

Aidyn's voice came over the earpiece. "We're all out. Elena, your mom is already making her way down the other side."

"Thank you," she whispered.

She swiped at the tears that prickled her eyes and picked up a stick. She ran it along the dirt in front of her to help her balance. Her heartbeat accelerated as they made their way down the mountain. She couldn't believe she was coming down for the last time. She was going to ask Aidyn to help them, but she didn't know he had already been planning it. That made her heart feel light. He cared enough for her to act quickly.

Every time fear threatened to weigh her down, she pushed it aside. No matter what happened, in time, it would still be better than living up there on the mountain married to a man she didn't love and letting him rut on her like a pig. Birthing babies she'd have to take care of and teach how to brew so they'd continue the cycle. When she had babies, she wanted them to play and be happy and grow up to be what they wanted to be.

Kent had told her that people picked what they wanted to do in other places. If it hadn't been for Kent's father paying for his college and getting Everett to let Kent come back if he wanted, Kent would never have gotten to leave like he did.

The only reason he came back was for his mom. But now, she was gone. Maybe Kent would leave one day too. She hoped he did. He was smart and he was nicer than the rest of them up there. Though he was mean to Lara last year. Out of frustration more than anything else. Maybe, one day, she'd be able to help Kent get off the mountain. Maybe.

She stepped onto the plateau they'd rested on before and waited. One by one they all appeared. The sky was lightening up and she glanced to the east to gauge the time.

"Sun will be up soon."

She began creeping along the path, more eager than ever to get off this mountain before everyone started waking up. Craig would be eager to hear her decision today and she figured he'd be up earlier than usual. It was a sneaky way to steal their recipe and even without the ick factor of having to have sex with him to conceive, the fact that he'd use her so callously to steal the family recipe was abhorrent. On top of that, she'd see her baby grow up but not be able to have a say in his or her upbringing. That wasn't something she'd be able to do. Not even for the promise of not having to marry someone she didn't want to marry.

Raised voices sounded from a distance and she froze. Fear stuck in her throat. Aidyn whispered, "Gotta make tracks. Someone's raised an alarm."

Adelaide bumped into her. "We've gotta go, Elena."

"Yeah." She swallowed and tried keeping her footing even. Tears threatened but she blinked them away. She sent up a silent prayer that her mom was alright and they'd all meet up in a little while.

Thrashing in the brush to her left caused her to gasp and freeze. Another raised voice from above and a deer jumped across the path in front of her and skittered off to the right.

She huffed out a breath and kept walking. Her knees were weak and shook slightly and she could feel her pulse pound in her neck. It felt like her heart struggled to beat just now.

Aidyn's breathing picked up a bit, she knew it was him. "I think we need to split up."

"Great idea. I'll go off to the left." Tate responded.

Adelaide said, "I'll stay with Elena."

Spencer then huffed out, "I'm going right."

Thrashing of the brush created too much noise and her heart felt like lead as she continued stumbling down the path. The sun now peeked above the mountain tops, lightening the sky. She could see more now and it was easier to make her way along the brush.

She whispered, "Adelaide, let's get off the path and go

through the brush. If we hear someone coming, duck down and sit tight."

"Roger."

Elena shook her head.

Adelaide said, "Sorry. Got it."

She'd have to ask them about Roger. She didn't know who he was.

The brush was thick here and more difficult to trudge through, but it offered them some cover. She and Adelaide were close to the same size, so they didn't break through the brush like a larger person or an animal did. She tripped on a rock and fell but jumped up right away and kept going.

"Are you alright?" Adelaide asked.

"Yes." She could feel blood trickling down her shin, but she'd deal with it later.

She looked ahead to see how far they had to go and saw the sun's rays glint off the trucks at the bottom. "Almost there."

Sounds from behind her caused her to look back. She saw someone moving in the brush then she heard Craig's voice. "They can't be far."

She dropped down to her knees and Adelaide did the same next to her. Elena slowly reached for the brush on either side of her and pulled it slowly together, so it didn't look like they'd made a nest. Adelaide did the same thing and they sat quietly. Except for her breathing. She couldn't get a good lung full of air. She was afraid to adjust her position. The thrashing came closer to them and she squeezed her eyes closed. More thrashing in the brush and a deer stood near her. It was huffing out sounds, likely it could smell her but was afraid of Craig and whoever else was with him. She kept her head down and waited for them to pass and hoped like hell they wouldn't trip on her and Adelaide.

Her heart beat so hard it almost hurt in her chest.

She could hear Craig now, he was a few yards above them. "Where the hell did they go? How many did you see?"

"I guess about three."

Stupid Ramsay. That's who that was. He was likely spying on her from across the center court. She should have guessed that was the case.

She sent up more prayers to let them escape this. Then she heard sickening thuds and punches and grunts and Aidyn's labored breathing, and the tears spilled from her eyes.

She started to move, but Adelaide lay a hand on her shoulder and pushed her down. She opened her eyes to Adelaide's and saw her shake her head. Adelaide fisted her left hand and lay it over her heart and mouthed, "Strong."

She slowly inhaled a deep breath. Strong. She needed to stay strong. The punching stopped and Aidyn's choppy breath said, "Get out now."

Adelaide grabbed her clothing by the shoulder and lifted her and they took off running. Sort of. They went as fast as they could down the mountain toward the trucks. The good news was if Craig was on this side of the mountain, he wasn't looking for her mom on the other side.

The brush thinned and they were able to move faster toward the bottom. Adelaide grabbed her hand, and they ran together to the bottom and across the road. Spencer was there, starting his truck. Tate was just running to his truck, but she didn't see Aidyn. She turned to go back but Adelaide held her tightly and said, "Keep going."

She sobbed but had no choice but to keep up with Adelaide. She was strong for a smaller woman.

As they ran across the road she pulled away and turned to see Aidyn's head as he ran down the mountain. She sobbed as she watched him, her heart in her throat.

He reached the bottom of the mountain and yelled, "Get in the trucks."

She opened the door of his truck and Adelaide all but pushed her inside, then jumped in the backseat.

Aidyn was the best sight she'd seen in a long time. He had blood on his face, but he was running. He jumped in his truck and started it up. Within a second he had it moving forward. "Everyone okay?"

One by one they replied, "Okay."

He turned and looked at her. "Elena?"

She nodded as tears streamed down her face. Blood ran from his nose and she remembered the things he called tissues in the compartment in front of her. She pushed the button and pulled some tissues from inside and handed them over.

He grinned and took them as he turned onto the road that would take them around the mountain.

35

He swiped at the blood dripping from his nose and navigated the road. The sun was filling the sky and visibility was good. Good enough that he wanted to be out of sight by the time that fucker Craig came to.

Adelaide dug around in the first aid kit in the back-seat. "How bad is it Aid?"

"It's slowing down."

He heard the package rip and she tapped him on the shoulder. "Here's a plug."

He shoved it into the nostril that was bleeding and navigated a corner.

Tate asked, "Everyone okay?"

Addy said, "Aidyn, Elena, and I are good."

Spencer replied. "All good."

Tate asked, "What happened back there, Aid?"

"Craig caught up to me. He had Ramsay with him. We had a scuffle. They're lying up there."

"Are they dead?"

Aidyn laughed. "No."

"Okay. As soon as we get around the mountain, I'm

going up partway to see if Grace needs help. Unless she's already at the bottom."

"Roger."

Elena looked at him. "Why do you say Roger?"

"It's a military term from the good old days. It means I understand or got it."

She nodded and he grinned. He couldn't wait to show her all the things. Everything. A fair. A farmer's market. A mall. Grocery stores and clothing stores and a hospital and doctors' offices. Though he hoped those were only for good reasons.

"I'm at the bottom of the mountain. I don't see Grace."

Elena sat forward and began scanning the area. She whispered, "I don't see her."

He leaned over and squeezed her hand. "We'll get her."

She squeezed his hand in return but didn't look at him. He pulled his truck to the edge of the parking lot where he'd been meeting Elena. He searched the area and couldn't see her. He opened his door but Adelaide said, "No. I'll go. You are not welcome. Certainly not if Craig has gotten back up the mountain."

Reluctantly he closed his door and they watched Adelaide strut across the street.

"She's brave."

"She is. Maya is too. They're cousins and have many similarities."

"Why don't you date one of them?"

His brows furrowed and he turned his head to look into her eyes.

"Because I don't want to. We all grew up together. Tate, Spencer, Adelaide, Maya, Henry, and me. Myles, Maya's twin brother, is coming next week. I've known them since

I was five. We were schooled together. Lived together sometimes. Sometimes just in close proximity with each other. We're friends and I love them. I'd give my life for any of them and they me."

"But she's brave and strong and confident."

"She is. They all are. But so are you, Elena."

"You two are sweet, but too much talking. I can't hear out here." Adelaide snarked and Elena threw her hands up to her face and he chuckled. "Nice to know I'm brave and strong though. Thank you, Elena."

"I'm sorry. I didn't mean to embarrass you."

Addy chuckled and then he could hear her breathing increase. "I've found her. Grace. Grace are you alright?"

"Yes. So tired."

"Okay, let me help you up."

Rustling sounds came over the earpieces and he continued to grip Elena's hand. She couldn't go running over there.

A gunshot sounded. "Son of a bitch. They're shooting at us."

Spencer and Tate both responded. "I'm on backup."

Return fire sounded and Aidyn scanned the bottom of the mountain for movement.

"Get down, Elena."

"What?"

"Down. Get down on the floor."

He moved the truck to the edge of the road and drove to meet Addy and Grace. He jumped from the truck and ran to help Addy. Grace was winded and moving slow. He picked her up and carried her the rest of the way. Addy ran ahead and opened the back door. He practically shoved her inside as Addy helped to pull her in and took off.

"I've got her. Back to the HOG."

"Roger."

Elena scrambled up from the floor and leaned between the driver's and passenger seats. "Mama. Are you alright?"

"That bastard shot at me."

"I know. Did you get hit?"

"No. But you can bet I'm pretty mad."

Elena laughed then and his heart felt lighter. "I'll bet you are."

The drive to the HOG wasn't far and he soon saw Tate's truck behind them. He pulled his card from his pocket and had it ready to scan when he got to the gate.

It opened and he zipped around the HOG and into the garage. Grace gasped in the back seat, and he locked eyes with her in the mirror. "It's alright. We're safe here."

He parked the truck and jumped out to help Grace from the cab. He helped her into the house and seated her at the dining room table. Lara was cooking something delicious already this morning and began pulling bottles of water from the refrigerator and coffee cups from the cupboard.

Elena sat next to her mom and took her left hand in both of hers. "Mama, this is Lara."

Grace looked into Lara's eyes. "Kent's sister, Lara?"

Lara frowned slightly. "Lara Vickers. It's nice to meet you."

Elena smiled. "Grace. Her name is Grace."

"It's nice to meet you, Grace. I have water here for you. Do you like tea or would you like to try coffee?"

"The coffee is pretty good, Mama, if you put creamer in it."

Grace's fingers shook as she picked up a bottle of water

and stared at it. The bottle crinkled in her hand as she turned it. "Who puts all this water in these little containers?"

He grinned. "It's done by machine. Maybe one day we'll go on a tour of a factory."

"A factory?"

"Where they bottle the water."

She struggled with the top. He picked it up and twisted it off for her, then handed it to her. He glanced at Elena. "What do you need, Elena?"

She skittered around the table to him, threw her arms around him and hugged him so tightly his heart felt light and free. He wrapped her in his arms and held her close. He pulled his comm unit from his ear, flicked the receiver off, and laid it on the table. Then he folded her into his body again.

36

She was so excited to show her mom a shower. And a toilet. And a faucet. It was fun watching her expressions at all the new discoveries. The women here were so sweet, they brought beautiful smelling soaps and lotions and shampoo and conditioner. She'd never in her life had conditioner for her hair and she couldn't believe how it made her hair feel.

Lara showed her a blow-dryer and then used a hot metal pole to curl her hair. Her hair was curled. Then she had her put lotion on her body and she felt so smooth and good and fresh. She looked in the mirror and couldn't believe the person looking back at her.

"Thank you, Lara. I've never...I don't recognize myself. I didn't know...Look my hair is shiny."

Lara laughed. "Your hair is beautiful. I'm glad Maya had clothes to fit you until we can get you to the store for your own."

She swung her head around. "I don't have any money. I can't..."

Lara waved her hand. "Aidyn said he's covering it. You can talk to him about it."

"I'm speechless...I mean I don't know what to say...It's too generous. How will I repay you for all of this?"

Lara pulled her in for a hug. "I'd say right now, the main thing is making sure your mom is healthy. From there, Aidyn and you will have a talk. The rest of us are happy you're here and we'll help you learn what you need to learn."

Lara turned to leave the bathroom and said, "Now, if you bring your dirty clothes out here, I'll show you how to wash them."

"Oh, I know how to...Wait, you don't use a wash bucket do you?"

Lara chuckled. "No. We have a washing machine."

Elena picked up her clothes and followed Lara out of the room. There was a small room next to the kitchen where there were two big metal machines. Lara opened one of the doors. "Put your clothes in here. Your mom's are already in here."

She pushed her clothes into the machine and Lara opened a big orange container and inside were little packets. "These are laundry pods. You put one in the washer with your dirty clothes."

"What does it do?"

"It's laundry detergent. It will help to clean your clothes."

She put it in with her clothes and Lara closed the door. "You push this button to turn it on. Then turn this dial one click. Then push this button."

The machine made a noise, and she jumped back. "What's happening?"

"It's filling with water." She stood and watched it for a

minute and a timer went off. "I have to pull the buns from the oven. I'll be in the kitchen when you're ready to come out."

She stood there mesmerized by the washing machine for a long time and shook her head. No way it would get all the dirt out. Sometimes she had to scrub grass stains pretty hard to get them out.

Her mom was in a bedroom across the house from where she and Aidyn were, but they each had their own bathrooms. Adelaide helped her mom shower, and they were doing something called a video chat with Adelaide's mom so she could diagnose her mom's condition. Elena eventually moved out to the kitchen and looked around. "Where's Aidyn?"

"I think he and Tate and Spencer are in a meeting in Tate's office."

"Okay." She watched Lara pull the buns from little metal cup things. "Can I help with something?"

"Sure. Tell me what you know how to cook."

"I can cook venison. Smoke it or fry it. I can make potatoes and carrots. I was never good at biscuits."

Lara smiled at her and stopped what she was doing. "How about this. I'll show you some cooking and you show me some cooking."

"Okay."

"So tonight I was going to make a big pork roast. We usually have a full time cook here, her name is Helissa, but she doesn't work weekends. So, I cook on the weekends. She usually leaves something in the refrigerator for us but she hasn't quite gotten the hang of cooking for four big men and that food doesn't last long in the fridge. There's always someone eating around here."

"Okay. I don't know how to make a roast."

"Good. I'll teach you."

Lara pulled a big package from the refrigerator and set it on the counter. It was laying on a tray and had clear wrap over it. Elena touched the wrap, and it was flexible. "I've never seen that before."

"It's called plastic wrap."

Lara used a knife and slit the plastic wrap open. "I'll let the roast bloom for a bit while we make the rub."

"Okay."

Lara opened a cupboard that was filled with spices and herbs, all in little glass containers with pretty labels. She was fascinated by all the varieties of spices. Some were ground and some were leaves and some were coarse ground. It was amazing. Lara told her which spices to pull out and she did that.

They worked in unison and Elena couldn't ever remember a time when life was so laid back. They weren't hurrying to pick spices or pull potatoes from the ground. They had everything they needed in glass jars or containers in the refrigerator. They worked but not like she'd always worked.

"Elena?"

She looked up to see Aidyn staring at her and she froze. The look on his face was different. He swallowed but stared. Finally Lara said, "She's beautiful isn't she?"

"Yes." It was hard to hear him. She bit her bottom lip because he was beginning to make her nervous. "Can you spare a minute to talk with some friends of mine?"

She looked around and didn't see anyone. "Yes." Then she remembered she was helping Lara. "Oh, is it alright, Lara?"

Lara's smile was brilliant. "Absolutely. I've got this."

She washed her hands like Lara showed her and

wiped them on the towel next to the sink. As she walked toward Aidyn, he kept staring. She looked down at her clothing. "These are Maya's."

"You look beautiful in them."

"I've never worn britches like these. Jeans they called them."

37

He pulled her to the conference room which was in the middle of the house and surrounded in glass. He pulled a chair out from the big table and motioned for her to sit down. They sat at an angle to each other at the end of the table.

"First of all. You are stunning, Elena. I thought you were pretty the first time I saw you. The first time I hugged you I thought all those baggy clothes you wore hid so much of your body. The first time I made love to you, I couldn't believe how good you felt. You fit against me perfectly. But, seeing you in clothing that shows off your shape like this, you take my breath away."

She swallowed and stared at him. "Thank you."

He grinned then leaned in and kissed her lips. Softly, sweetly and it was perfect. Then he leaned back and took a deep breath.

"I have friends back home who I thought could help you. Emersyn is a badass operative like Addy and Maya. She owns a sister company of ours, RAPTOR. She's also Tate's cousin."

"Oh. Okay." Her eyebrows bunched slightly.

"Emersyn's husband is a doctor. Chase Nicholas. Chase is also a scientist. He's been developing some serum for the past few years to help people. I thought with your elixir, he could help you brew it and develop it so you can sell it to make money and help people. There are regulations you'd have to follow, and he has a lab you could use. He would help you with all of it and all the money would be yours."

"Oh. Okay. So I wouldn't be with you anymore?" Her eyes welled with tears.

He took her hands in his. "I'd go with you. If you want me to. I want you to have a fresh start in life. If you don't want to do that with me, I understand." His voice cracked at the end and he took a deep breath. He had to give her the opportunity to leave him if she wanted.

"I want to be with you. I love you. I understand you need me to work to make money. I've always worked. I'll work hard for you."

He sat back. "No. No. No." He scooted his chair closer. "I don't need you to work for me. As a matter of fact, I don't care if you work at all. I work. I can support both of us if you don't want to work. But I thought this would be a way for you to be independent so you never feel stuck again."

Grace came from her bedroom and walked into the conference room. "May I join you?"

"Yes, Grace. I was just telling Elena about my friends Emersyn and Chase Nicholas."

He explained to Grace about Chase's lab, and she nodded. Grace looked at Elena. "Do you want to keep brewing, Elena? It will be different, but I'll be with you. I'll help you. I have to make money to live in this world."

He watched Elena stare at her mom for a long time. "Mama, I'll brew with you if you want me too."

He wasn't convinced her heart was in it and he pondered that a moment. The conference room phone rang and he slid the speaker down toward them. "This will be Emmy and Chase."

"Hello. This is Aidyn."

"Hi, Aidyn, this is Emmy and Chase."

"It's good to hear your voice again, Emmy. Hi, Chase."

"Hi, Aidyn. I understand you've all met with some interesting events down there."

"We sure have." He reached over and took Elena's hand in his. "I have two of the most interesting people here to speak with you about their elixir. Elena and Grace Dorsey."

He sat back as Chase spoke about his lab and explained some regulations which he knew they didn't understand. It would likely be the hardest part of them brewing in the end. It was the hardest part of everything everyone did. Deal with regulations that usually seemed stupid and unnecessary.

Chase ended the call, "Well, Aidyn will bring you back here and I'll show you the lab. We'll talk about supplies and how to get you started. I understand Elena, you took a sample from your latest batch. Aidyn mailed it this morning so we can test it and see what it actually does. How does that sound?"

"Good." Elena said.

Grace's smile, for the first time since he'd met her early this morning, was bright. "That sounds wonderful Dr. Nicholas."

Chase laughed. "Ah, we're going to be colleagues. Please call me Chase."

They ended the call and Grace burst out laughing. "I kind of have a job. I'm forty-four and have my first job!"

He laughed with her but noticed Elena was more subdued.

"How would you ladies like to go for a ride and see the town? We have time before supper is ready."

Grace smiled genuinely. "I'd love to, Aidyn, and thank you so much. But I'm exhausted and would like to rest for a while if you don't mind. You two go and spend time together."

Grace stood, kissed Elena's head. "You look beautiful, Elena." She nodded at him and exited the conference room.

He leaned forward and took Elena's hands in his. "How about it, Elena. Can I show you the town?"

"Yes. I'd love that."

He stood and pulled her up, then he pulled her in for a hug. "Are you worried about all the changes?"

He felt her chest expand and deflate, then she nodded her head. But he didn't believe her.

Pulling her to the door, they exited through the kitchen. "Lara, I'm taking Elena out to see the town."

"Fantastic. I'll see you both in a while."

They strode to his truck and he helped her into the passenger seat. Passing in front of the truck, he stretched his shoulders and tried to release some of the stress that had gathered as he watched Elena shrink back during the phone call.

They left the HOG and he thought a drive in the country would be nice. He hadn't seen a lot of the area since he'd been here. There were some horse farms along the road behind the HOG.

He let her have her silence and as they neared a farm

her eyes rounded at the beautiful horses running along the fence with them. She giggled at the foals jumping with their mamas and she clapped her hands when she saw puppies running in the field with them.

He laughed with her and took her hand in his. He turned them into town and drove down Main Street. He showed her some of the stores. "That's Divine Designs. Lara's best friend, Shianne owns it."

He drove further down the street. "That's Lara's bakery."

"I've peeked in the windows of her bakery. More than once."

He smiled at her. "Little rebel."

She shrugged.

Then he drove past Bloomin' Lovely. "That's the flower shop."

"They sell flowers?"

"Yes. I suppose other things too."

"Can I see?"

He looked into her eyes. "Sure."

He pulled into a parking lot and turned the truck around. When he pulled up to Bloomin' Lovely, she leaned forward and looked out the windshield.

Stepping from the truck he strode around to help her out and she saw two long tent-like structures in the back. "What are those?"

"I believe those are the greenhouses."

"They aren't green."

"Ah, greenhouses, as they pertain to gardening, are where you start seeds and get them ready for planting or potting."

She stared into his eyes for a long time. "May I see the greenhouses?"

"Let's go see."

He took her hand and meandered among the many plants and pots of flowers outside. She looked at everything and smelled most of them. Once inside, he asked the clerk if they could see the greenhouses. "She's never been in one and would like to see it."

"Oh, sure. We don't mind. Go right on through that door."

He grinned at Elena and led her to the door. As they stepped into the greenhouse the smell of fresh wet dirt and flowers surrounded them. Elena walked along and looked at all the plants. She touched them, put her finger in the soil, smelled the flowers and looked at the watering system. A lady was working toward the back and Elena approached her. "Hi. May I ask a couple of questions?"

"Oh, of course."

"How long have you been working here?"

"I've been here around fifteen years now."

"Wow. That's wonderful. What do you like best about working here?"

"I love that I'm in nature. Every day. There's always something different to tend to and I love watching them grow. They're all my babies."

"I can see that. Thank you."

Elena turned to him and smiled. "I'm ready when you are."

His brows bunched but he followed her from the store and to the truck. After they got in, he started the truck but didn't move it.

"You'd rather grow plants, wouldn't you?"

She slowly turned to him. "I would. But I don't want to disappoint you."

That was a sucker punch. "Elena. Honey, I'm not

disappointed. Not in you. Not in what you think you want to do. It's your life, baby."

Tears gathered in her eyes. "But I want you to be in it."

"I am. I will be. What you do for a living doesn't matter to me."

"But you made plans with your friends."

"No, I offered you and your mom an opportunity to work with them. If you don't want to, you should grow plants. And if you decide you don't want to grow plants, do something else."

"Really?"

"Yes. Really. I'm serious."

He brushed her tears from her cheeks and softly kissed her lips.

"I love you, Elena. I don't love your job. Do you understand me?"

"Yeah."

38

Elena slid into bed as Aidyn showered. It reminded her of shower sex and she got excited. She squeezed her thighs together. As she pondered whether to join him, she heard the shower turn off.

Aidyn exited the bathroom naked as the day he was born. Handsome. Strong. He had muscles and muscles and muscles. His body was firm but she enjoyed touching him.

He grinned at her. "Staring?"

"Yes."

He strode to the opposite side of the bed and pulled the covers back, exposing her body to him. "Damn you're sexy, Elena."

She didn't feel embarrassed. He looked at her with such lust in his eyes. He leaned forward and grabbed her ankles and dragged her across the bed. She laughed. Then he spread her legs open and started on her right foot and lay soft wet kisses on her toes. He moved up the top of her foot, then her ankle then up her leg. His kisses felt good. She liked watching his lips touch her skin. He kissed up her thigh and then his tongue licked right up her privates. She gasped and froze. She lifted up on her elbows as he lifted his head slightly and grinned. "Nobody ever licked your pussy Elena?"

She shrugged. "Not like that."

He licked her again and again. Each time his tongue plunged deeper into her tissues. He found that spot she liked and he circled it with his tongue. She dragged in a breath as he softly touched her with his finger. He circled that spot, then slid his finger down and slowly pushed it inside of her. She watched it disappear inside of her but she couldn't move. Never in her life.

He pulled his finger out and slid it back in then his tongue licked her spot again. She lay back and slid her hands into his sexy hair. She felt his head bob up and down as he licked her. His finger probed in and out. The many sensations were incredible. She didn't know what she wanted to concentrate on first.

He added pressure to her spot, then he sucked her into his mouth. Her knees shook and her body felt pressure and then she felt the white-hot release and she gasped, "Aidyn."

"I love it when you come, Elena."

He finished licking her, then kissed down her other leg. Once he'd kissed her leg he moved up and kissed her belly. His tongue swirled around her belly button then he kissed up her torso to her left breast. He kissed it and sucked it into his mouth and flicked her nipple with his tongue and as if she hadn't come already, she felt it build again.

He moved his mouth to her other breast and repeated his motions and she couldn't breathe.

Then he looked into her eyes. His hazel eyes were

darker just now. He scooted up and kissed her lips, softly. Then he kissed to her ear and his tongue slid around the shell of her ear. His hand moved his penis to her entrance, and he slowly entered her. And it. Was. Glorious.

He moved in and out, then lifted her legs up. "Put your feet across my back baby."

She did as he asked, and he slid in deeper. She sighed. So did he.

Then they moved in unison. She felt the pressure build again and wanted the release so she moved faster and he took her cue and moved faster too. It didn't take them long and both of them gasped the other's name and stiffened as their orgasms hit like a wave and slowly slid back to sea.

He kissed her ear. "My God, Elena, I love you. I love making love with you. I love being with you."

"I love you too, Aidyn."

She kissed his cheek, then licked the edge of his ear and he huffed out a breath. "So precious."

She giggled and he kissed her cheek.

They cleaned up and snuggled into bed. It was only her second time spending the night in his arms but she couldn't see how she'd ever get tired of this.

"I love spooning with you."

"What's spooning?" She giggled.

"This. Your back to my front and my arms wrapped around you. It's called spooning."

"That's funny."

"When you put two spoons together like this, they fit perfectly together. That's where the name came from."

"Oh." She smiled and closed her eyes. "Aidyn?"

"Hmm."

"You didn't use protection."

"You said you didn't have a disease."

"I don't."

"Hmm."

"But what about babies?"

"Hmm. What about them?"

"What if I get pregnant."

"I'll hope for a boy. But I'll love a little girl too."

She let herself relax. "I'll hope for a girl. But I'll love a little boy."

He chuckled in her ear and it vibrated throughout her body.

She drifted off to sleep dreaming sweet thoughts of life with Aidyn and babies and flowers and so much love in their house. It was wonderful. Until it wasn't.

BANG!

He sat bolt upright then jumped from bed and dressed so fast she didn't know what he was doing. He pulled a gun from the bedside table and ran to the door. "Stay here."

He closed the door behind him, and she got up and dressed.

She rummaged around to find her shoes and heard more loud bangs outside. It sounded like someone was trying to get into the house. Staying in here was scary and she bet her mom was so worried. But Aidyn told her to stay here.

BANG!

She jumped when she heard the sound and she heard Tate yell, "Stay in your rooms."

She could hear voices. She sat in the armchair across the room and hugged herself as she waited to see what happened. Her mind ran wild, but what she knew was Craig was pissed off, and he wasn't going to let her and her mom go without a fight. There was no one up there to brew now. With them gone, their way of making money was gone. She made a huge mistake thinking about a life away from the mountain. She'd been seduced by a townie man and Craig was going to make someone pay.

39

Aidyn stood in the living room as bullets hit the windows. Luckily, they'd gone with bullet-proof glass, but even that wasn't able to withstand constant barrages of bullets.

Tate was on the phone with the sheriff and if they got here in time, they'd arrest and jail whoever was out there.

Craig was too much of a coward to come down himself, so he'd sent the flunkies down.

Sirens sounded, coming closer. The old pickup truck they drove could be heard driving away.

He ran toward the garage. "I'm after them."

Spencer was right behind him. "I'm with you."

They jumped in his truck and took off out of the gate. The taillights faded around a corner and Aidyn turned to head them off from the opposite direction. "Tell Tate where they are. He can tell the sheriff."

Spencer called Tate and relayed the information while Aidyn watched the road for debris and animals.

Spencer rolled his window down to listen for the truck. It was much easier when it was quiet outside.

"Spence, call Henry. He and Maya can cut them off so they can't go back up the mountain."

While he dialed, Aidyn turned toward the road close to the tree where he and Elena met. No headlights were visible, so he moved toward the construction site and the next road. There were three on this side of the mountain.

Spencer's phone rang and he tapped the speaker icon. "It's Henry. We've got this road blocked by the base. They'll have to go up the middle road."

Spencer replied, "Okay. We're heading there now." He shook his head, "I should have brought my truck. We could have blockaded the road."

"We still can. We'll use my truck. We can hide in the brush."

He pulled his truck across the road. He and Spencer jumped out and ran across the road to crouch in the shadows and watch.

The revving of a nearby engine made him turn his head.

Spencer drew his weapon. "I'm shooting out their tires."

The truck's headlights came closer. Aidyn took a few deep breaths to calm himself. Here they were, the repercussions he expected when he'd planned to bring Elena down.

The truck screeched to a halt just before turning up the road.

Several rounds of gunfire came from the old truck and sparks flew as they hit his vehicle. Spencer took aim at the tires on the old Ford. The BRR turned in their direction and returned fire.

Aidyn jumped behind the building but got in a few shots. The BRR exited their vehicle from the opposite side. He could see the brush move, but nothing further. Shooting ceased and he slipped around the back of the building to find Spencer on the other side.

"Do you see anything?"

"No, but I don't think they went up. I think they're waiting us out. Two of them."

Sirens approached. He pulled his phone out and called the police department. It rang once. "Glen Hollow Police Department."

"It's Aidyn Dunbar with GHOST. We have blocked the middle road and are engaged with the BRR. You have an officer approaching. Tell them extreme caution."

He didn't wait for confirmation before he hung up. There, he'd seen movement. He tapped Spencer's shoulder and pointed. Spencer nodded. "Got it."

Spencer took aim at their hiding spot while he scrambled from the shadows of the building to a few yards away where an old phone booth had been turned into a free library. Shots bounced off the pavement near him, but he dove behind the small structure. The squad car turned down a side street. He peered around his cover and a shot whizzed above his head. The glass shattered and rained down on him.

He scooted behind the library and took a few deep breaths.

He saw one of the Glen Hollow officers scramble behind a building down the side street. Spencer called out to him. "You good?"

"Yeah. You?"

"Yeah."

"Officers approaching from the north."

"Roger."

Roger. It made him think of Elena. He prayed no

shady shit was going down at the house. Tate and Addy were there, and the HOG was reasonably secure.

The officer scrambled across to his side of the street. He watched the officer's progress and hoped he or she wouldn't mistake him for one of the BRR.

The officer crept along the side of the building toward him. A shot rang out but missed its target.

Spencer returned fire and he heard it hit. The groan and thud of someone falling was hard to mistake. That left one.

He peered around the opposite side of the little library from where Spencer hid; the brush moved in the direction of his truck.

"Spencer?"

"Yep."

Aidyn scrambled to Spencer's side.

Spencer pointed to the shaking brush. "They're together right now."

Then one of the BRR let out a roar. "You fuckers!"

Bullets hit the building, the pavement, the little library. Spencer raised his gun and so did Aidyn. He took aim where the bullets came from and squeezed the trigger. The return barrage of bullets stopped.

The officer ran to their location. "Are you both okay?" Officer Gordon knelt behind him.

"Yep, we're good. Are you alright?"

"Yes. The sheriff is at your house right now."

"You'll want him to join us here. We shot both of them."

"Are they dead?"

"I don't know."

Brush began moving down from the mountain in several locations. "Heads up." He warned.

A man yelled out. "Stop. No more. Let us bring them up the mountain."

It sounded like Kent.

He called out. "Kent? Is that you?"

"Yes. No more shooting. We call truce."

Spencer turned his head. "Can we trust them?"

"I don't know." Could they trust them?

"Kent, we need reassurances on your truce."

The sounds of voices talking reached their ears but not actual words.

Slowly the brush moved. He raised his gun, and so did Spencer and Officer Gordon.

Kent stepped onto the road; his hands were up. He stopped in the center of the road looking in their direction.

"I'm here to ensure our truce. I'll stay here until they get Ramsay and Brenner up the mountain."

"What do you think Spencer?"

"I'll keep sights on him. Officer Gordon, how do you want to proceed?"

"I'll be honest, I don't know."

Aidyn holstered his gun. "I'll go and stand with Kent."

"Aidyn, what if they shoot?"

"They'll shoot Kent too."

He slowly stood and held his hands in the air. "I'm coming to stand with you Kent."

He stepped from the shadows and locked eyes with Kent. One twitch and he'd pull his weapon, but Spencer would already have him shot.

His stomach tightened and his lungs refused to expand enough for deep breaths. His steps were slow and sure as he neared the road. Kent turned his head slightly. "Go ahead and move them. No shady shit."

The rustling of the brush broke the silence.

He nodded to Kent as he approached, and they stared at each other for a long time. Kent broke the silence between them.

"Why did Elena give me her cabin?"

"She was grateful you offered to help her." He couldn't say 'marry her'—those words wouldn't come out of his mouth.

Kent chuckled. "Right." He took a deep breath. "A cabin is so much better than a wife and kids."

Aidyn's jaw clenched. This close he could see the resemblance with Lara. What a shame they didn't have a relationship. They were siblings.

Kent's next words came on a whisper. "Are you going to marry her?"

"Not that it's any of your business, but yes."

"Well, you've made it my business since you've shot two of our people, taken our brewer, and the only other person on the mountain who could teach anyone else to brew. You've disturbed our way of life in the most profound way, and you stand before me, snarking out some 'not that it's any of your business' bullshit."

"Your people wouldn't have been shot if they hadn't shot at us first. Elena and Grace didn't want to stay up there and if you're placing blame, blame your president for trying to force a marriage and kids on a woman who has always done what was asked of her. Talk about punishing someone who never did a cross thing to you. So, no, I am not to blame. Your president and his hate are to blame."

Kent inhaled deeply and let it out slowly. "I know you're right." He brushed the hair from his eyes by dipping his head and using his bicep to move it. "I tried talking to Craig. He's blinded by rage now. Though we all know up there that he wanted his father to step down so he could govern. He's a conundrum. And he's feeling desperate. Now, his desperation is at an all-time high. We have nothing to trade now."

"It seems you need to remove him as president since he's not rational."

"We've never done that."

"First time for everything."

Kent's jaw tightened. "I don't know if Gerard will do that."

"Who's Gerard?"

Kent took a deep breath once again. "Gerard Weston is Craig's brother-in-law and the vice president. Craig and Hanalore don't have children, so Gerard was named as Craig's closest relative. Jasiah Weston, Gerard and Lilianna's son, is secretary."

"Are they filled with hate as well?"

"No." He shook his head. "They want peace like the rest of us."

Aidyn's eyes widened. "You want peace? You made Lara's life a veritable hell last fall."

"I know. I was frustrated." Kent dipped his gaze as he spoke. "But, after it all shook out...my parents are dead now, I don't want all of this hate. I came back because I love the mountain life. We were peaceful, but I wanted to make life better. My dad said he'd send me to college to learn how to do that. I hated it at college. But I stuck it out and learned. When I came back, Lara had her bakery, and I was back on the mountain with nothing."

"It seems like you have nothing now. You had parents before. For the record, Lara didn't have that much. Her father was gone up on the mountain with you and your mom. Lara's mom was addicted to the elixir and Keaton kept her addicted, so he had a reason to come up the mountain and see you and your mom. Lara didn't have all you thought she had."

"Yeah." He nodded slowly.

Someone hollered down from the woods. "Kent, let's go."

He called back, "I'll be up in a while."

Aidyn lowered his arms. "Now what?"

Kent swallowed. "I don't know."

40

Elena sat on the sofa, her mom next to her. There were three large matching sofas in this room. Plush brown leather and soft as could be. Still, she couldn't get comfortable. Tate and Adelaide were in the office and she couldn't go back to bed until she knew Aidyn was alright. Her stomach was a mess. Lara offered her food, and she just couldn't. She did sip the water from the weird plastic bottle, though. She was used to working all day every day and today, or yesterday as it was now close to five in the morning, she hadn't done enough physical labor. She'd have to find something to do around here if they stayed.

She stood and paced again for the fifth or sixth time. Lara saw her from the kitchen.

"Elena, do you want to help me make breakfast?"

"Yes. Thank you. I need to do something."

Lara pulled eggs from the refrigerator. Those she knew how to make; they did have chickens up on the mountain.

"If you pull a bowl from the cupboard, we'll scramble them."

She did as she was told, happy for something to do.

The door opened behind her as she cracked the first egg. She whirled around to see Aidyn. She dropped the egg in the bowl and ran to him. He scooped her up in his arms.

"Oh my God, I've been so worried. Are you alright? Do you need anything? What happened?"

He kissed her lips and she kissed him right back. She squeezed him tightly. He chuckled and the vibrations rumbled through her body. Spencer came in behind Aidyn and she waved, but didn't want to let Aidyn go.

He squeezed her then set her on the ground but kept his arm around her.

Tate and Adelaide came in from the office, her mother trailing behind them, and the kitchen door opened once more and the two team members she hadn't met yet entered.

Aidyn introduced them. "Henry and Maya, this is Elena," he gestured to her mother, "and Elena's mom, Grace."

Elena's cheeks flushed hot as Maya grinned. She was still wearing her clothes. "Thank you for loaning me something to wear."

Maya nodded. "Happy to help."

Henry nodded and went to the refrigerator. He pulled a bottle of water out and cracked it open.

Tate stood at the big table. "Let's sit and talk about what happened. Then we'll talk about next steps."

Elena noticed that Lara had taken over cracking the eggs. "I'm sorry. Let me finish this."

Aidyn kissed the top of her head as he passed her, and she was finally able to lower her shoulders and relax a little.

Lara handed her a funny tool. "Now you use this. It's a whisk. Add a bit of milk to the eggs and whisk them all together." She looked at the whisk and grinned. "I saw a picture of one of these in a book." She put it in the bowl and stirred it.

Lara chuckled. "Put movement into it. Like this." She spun her hand quickly and Elena mimicked her movement.

The eggs broke up and the milk stirred in. It was fun, much more efficient than a fork or spoon, and she burned off some energy too.

Lara then showed her how to work the stove for the scrambled eggs and she managed rather well. She wasn't ready to do it on her own just yet, but she was learning.

She carried two big bowls of eggs to the table, Lara brought fresh biscuits and bacon. And they all filled their coffees or waters or orange juice. She'd never had orange juice before. Her mom, either. They grinned at each other as they ate their first piece of bacon. Their diet usually consisted of venison or squirrel, eggs, biscuits, and potatoes or carrots. Tea and water were the only liquids they had, besides the elixir, which she didn't drink because of the risk of addiction.

When they were mostly finished, Tate asked, "Aidyn and Spencer, tell us what happened out there."

She watched Aidyn's face as he retold the activities of the night. When he mentioned that Ramsay and Brenner had been shot, she felt bad. Her mom was the only one who voiced the truth. "They were being trained to hate and be hateful. It's too bad their parents didn't have more influence on them. They hung on to Craig and his negative talk."

Her mom's eyes darted to hers and she nodded

slightly.

Aidyn said, "Hopefully they'll be alright and change their behavior."

Her mom responded. "They'll die. Depending on where they were shot. There's no doctor up there and Craig won't allow them to come down for help. Elenor does the best she can and she's better than most. But she can't do much more than remove the bullets and stitch them up. Sometimes the elixir will help a bit but it's not good for repairing tissue. It helps with heart ailments and breathing issues."

Elena listened to her mom's matter-of-fact description and remembered all the times her mom warned her of their limitations and the problems facing them up there on the mountain. Though she was born on the mountain, her mother had told her what they left behind a lot. When her mom married her dad, it was a love match and that kept her mom up on the mountain, but late at night in their cabin, her parents often discussed the pitfalls they faced up there.

Aidyn reached over and covered her hands with his. She turned to look into his eyes. "Do you think Kent was earnest?"

Aidyn's eyes stared into hers. She felt comforted by his calm. "I do. He wants change."

"Does he think Gerard will overthrow Craig?"

"He wasn't sure of that."

She looked across the table at her mom. Her mom's response was to shrug. "Gerard's a good man. Liliana is a good woman. They'll do what's right, but they may not feel overthrowing Craig is right. They may simply work to limit him in some way."

"Mama, there is no way to limit Craig. He'll work

behind their backs to countermand everything Gerard and Liliana try to do."

Aidyn cleared his throat. "We have a meeting this afternoon at the Sheriff's Department with Kent and Gerard. Tate, this is a great time to come up with some concessions for them. If they depose Craig, we'll allow them to come down and work. They can live up there but come down and earn money to support themselves. They'd have to abide by our laws. But we may be able to find a peace with them and not force them into anything that will make them rebel."

Tate nodded. "That's a great idea, Aidyn. What type of work can most of them do?"

He turned to her. She glanced at her mom briefly before answering Tate. "They can farm. Believe it or not, we're all hard workers. We've eked out a life up there with little. Most of the men are great builders. They can make the most intricate things from wood and supplies found in the forest and on the ground. The hunters would be great hunting guides. They can track deer better than the average man. The women right now are largely caretakers, sewers, and cooks."

Tate nodded. "Those are great ideas. There are plenty of farmers here who need help. There are plenty of builders around here who need help. Our daycares are always in need of help."

Tate took a deep breath. "I'm going to put together some ideas to amend the Treaty."

Elena stood and began clearing the table of plates and silverware. When she came back for more, Aidyn placed his hand on her back. "After we're finished meeting with Tate, can we talk?"

She studied his face for a minute. "Sure."

41

Tate tapped his pen on the sheet of paper in front of him. "I think we have a great list here. Let's pray we can broker a deal. It's for the benefit of all of us. I'll call the mayor now and tell him what's up and see if he'll call an emergency session of the town council today to get some approvals and clarifications."

Aidyn stood. "It sounds like the best way for all of this to work out. But, of course, they're the ones who have to venture down the mountain and change their way of life."

"That's true."

"I've got to have a chat with Elena. Then I need a nap before the meeting."

"We all should rest up a bit. Thanks for all your help, Aidyn."

He nodded and left to go in search of Elena. He checked the bedroom and found it empty. He meandered out to the kitchen and found Lara making a grocery list. "Hey, I know you do so much for us around here and I hope you know we all appreciate it."

She smiled. "I enjoy doing it. Honestly."

"I was going to ask one more thing."

She smiled and pointed to her list. "I'll add it to the list."

"Grace and Elena need clothes and shoes and..." He waved his hands. "You know, girly things. But I'm afraid it isn't safe for them to go out right now. Things are uncertain."

Lara nodded. "You know my bestie owns a dress shop, right? She's all about clothes and girly things." She waved her hands just as he had, and he chuckled. "Okay. Right."

"I thought I'd invite her to come out this afternoon and take measurements and make a list of things they need. How do you feel about that?"

"I love it." He clapped his hands and allowed himself to breathe a bit. "I wasn't sure how to handle this."

Lara giggled. "We've got you. I'll call Shianne."

He knocked on the top of the counter. "Thanks. Where's Elena?"

"I think she's in with her mom."

He turned toward Grace's room. He knocked softly and Elena opened the door.

"Hi."

She smiled sweetly. "Hi."

"Is this a good time to talk?"

"Yes."

Grace lay on her bed with her back to the headboard. She had a doctor's appointment on Monday, and they'd start her on medication which would hopefully help her feel better.

He took Elena's hand and led her outside. He strode to the picnic table where he usually had his coffee and sat with his butt on the table, his feet on the seat. He patted the table next to him and she sat alongside him.

He pointed to the mountain. "I'd sit here in the morning with my cup of coffee and stare at the mountain and wonder what you were doing."

She smiled. "I'd sit, right about there..." She pointed to a spot. "And wonder what you were doing down here."

He chuckled. "If things work out with the Treaty today and we find common ground and a real truce, what do you want to do?"

"I don't see that I have anything to do with it."

"I mean." He turned to face her. "Do you want to stay here if that's the case?"

She laid her right hand on his cheek. "No, Aidyn. My mama's going to work with Chase. Or at least see if there is something she can do with the elixir. She'll be alone if I don't go with her, and I thought you were coming with us."

He softly brushed a stray lock of dark hair from her cheek and tucked it behind her ear. "Elena, I want to be with you. But I want you to be sure. This, I'm sure... must be overwhelming. It'll be a lot of change."

"So will going back up there. And, honestly, if I did, it would be harder for them to change and old patterns would stick."

He smiled. "You're so wise."

She giggled. "Not sure about that. But I want you to know, because you seem unsure. I want to be with you, Aidyn. If I closed my eyes right now and pictured my future, I see you."

He kissed the tip of her nose. "When I close my eyes, I see you. Always."

He kissed her soft lips and pulled her head to his shoulder to hug her.

"So, this afternoon, Lara's friend Shianne will be coming over to fit you and your mom for new clothes. Don't worry about cost. Just tell her what you want. Shianne and Lara will get it for you. I'm sorry you have to wait for a while to go shopping yourself, but it isn't safe right now and I have to be at the meeting."

"It's okay. But, Aidyn, you don't have to spend a lot of money on me. I can make do. Mama too. We're used to it."

"I know you are. Look, I've worked all my life too. Helping my mom out on the gun range. Then the military. Then I came back and began working for GHOST. I've always lived in a GHOST house or on base. I've made money but not spent much. Just my shot up old truck in there, which I'll need to replace. But I'm solid and it's my way of helping you both with a fresh new start."

"Thank you."

"I do have to warn you though. Shianne—is a lot. I mean, she's a handful."

"Okay. Do you mean she won't like us?"

"Oh honey, she'll love you both just fine. She's just a flurry of activity and talking."

"Oh."

He chuckled. "You'll see. But if she overwhelms you, just know it's temporary."

"Okay." She chuckled. She turned then and faced the mountain, and they sat in silence for a long while watching the varying colors of the trees. The sun felt good today, it was nearly sixty and they both sat out there without jackets. It was peaceful.

Aidyn yawned. "I need a nap."

She giggled. "Me too."

He stepped down and took her hand in his. They walked together into the HOG and to the bedroom. He lay on top of the bed and pulled her into his body.

"Spooning." She giggled.

"Spooning."

42

Elena and Grace stood near the kitchen island as Shianne giggled and squealed in a flurry of movement around them. "What's your favorite color? Ohmygawd, you have the prettiest green eyes. How about green? Do you like green? This is so exciting."

"Shianne. Gawd, settle down. You'll scare the both of them. To be honest, I'm a little freaked right now." Lara laughed.

Shianne tucked her short dark hair behind her ear. "I'm sorry. But this is a dream come true. I'm a personal shopper for two beautiful ladies. I mean, we dream of this stuff. Right?"

"I don't." Lara quipped.

Shianne turned back to her and huffed out a breath. "I'm sorry, Elena. I'm not trying to freak anyone out. But as a boutique owner this is my dream come true. To be able to personally shop for someone. And you, my gawd, you're gorgeous. Petite, long dark hair, gorgeous green eyes. Oh, I simply can't wait to bring clothing back for you."

"Okay." What was she supposed to say?

"Aren't you excited?"

Her cheeks burned and she could feel her chest heat and her underarms were warm. She shrugged. "I've always made do with what I had and...this is all something entirely different than anything I've ever experienced. These clothes are just fine."

She looked down at her borrowed long-sleeved t-shirt and jeans. "I mean, they aren't mine, but something like this is fine."

Shianne's lips turned down for a split second, then she turned them up. "Okay. Well, I can absolutely get you some jeans. You'll need those too. But I'll get you some other things too. What size bra do you wear?"

Ugh. She was burning up this time. She glanced at Lara and tried pleading with her eyes.

"Shianne. Can we be less enthusiastic and more professional? Honey, this is all new for Elena. And, likely overwhelming."

"I'm sorry." Shianne grabbed both of her hands together. "I'm sorry. I'll curb my excitement."

She stood straight and swallowed.

Elena took a deep breath. "I've never had a bra. I wore my dad's old tank tops."

"Okay. Then we'll measure you."

Shianne reached into a bag and pulled out a flexible ribbon with numbers on it. "Okay, hold your arms out like you're going to fly."

She held her arms out and Shianne reached around her and pulled the tape under her breasts. She wrote something down on a piece of paper. Then she lifted the ribbon and ran it over her breasts, then wrote something down.

She looked at the inside neckline of Maya's shirt. She

looked at the label on the inside of Maya's jeans then she measured her feet. It was embarrassing.

"Okay. Now you, Grace." Her mom reluctantly traded places with her and Elena wondered how to get rid of her headache. Up on the mountain she'd use Basil and Chamomile and make a tea. She padded to the cupboard with the spices in it and wondered if she could find those things in there. Lara quietly sidled up to her.

"Shianne is a good person. She's just very excited."

"I can tell."

Lara chuckled. "Do you have a headache?"

"Yes."

"I'll get you some aspirin."

"I don't know what aspirin is. I usually drink chamomile and basil tea."

"Aspirin is medicine in a pill that relieves headaches."

"Oh."

She looked at the clock on the stove; it said three forty-five. Aidyn had been gone for two hours. She'd done very little today but she was tired again.

Lara came back into the kitchen, poured her hot water from the tea kettle they'd pulled out for her and her mama to have tea, and laid two white pills on the counter. "These are aspirin. They'll take your headache away. Sit down and have your tea and try to relax. I'll shoo Shianne out the door as soon as she's finished measuring your mom. She'll be excited to shop anyway."

"Thank you, Lara. You've helped Mom and me so much and we do appreciate it."

Lara turned and leaned against the counter and crossed her arms. She grinned as she watched Shianne measuring her mom. "You know, you and your mom have helped us all too. I'm fascinated with how you lived up there. I grew up with modern conveniences. You didn't and look how well you're adapting. Plus, you're teaching me some things too. I didn't know that chamomile and basil got rid of headaches. But I'll order some herbs and try it to see if it works."

"You order herbs? From where?"

"The internet."

Elena's eyebrows rose into her hairline, and she took a deep breath. "Okay."

"How did you get them?"

"I grow them." She sipped her tea. "I mean, I used to."

"You should keep doing that. Do you know how much money you could make selling herbs? Good lord there's so many people looking for natural remedies to everyday things."

"Really?"

"Yes. Selling them fresh you'd make a killing."

She swallowed and let her mind turn this over. She wanted to grow plants, but she meant herbs and things she used. She liked flowers but up on the mountain it was hard to grow them and she didn't have the time up there to keep a flower garden. It was all she could do to keep her potatoes and carrots. Keep the firewood stacked up and gather herbs for the elixir.

"Lara. Do you have books on herbs and where they sell them?"

"Okay. Let me set you up. Sit at the counter, I'll be right back."

Elena poured a bit more water into her teacup, then settled onto a barstool. Shianne was now measuring her mom's breasts and she saw her mom glance at her once then look away. Her mom was sixteen years older than she was and had never had her breasts measured. But she handled it well.

Lara came back into the kitchen with a rectangle box. "This is my tablet." She set it up on the counter, it had a stand that it stood against, and she touched the screen and it lit up. "This is an electronic tablet." She tapped a few times. "This is the internet. From here you can scroll and find anything in the world you want." She pointed to a white bar at the top. "Type in herbs and you can find anything."

She tapped the white bar and a little box with the letters of the alphabet popped up and she typed herbs. Lara then showed her where to tap and a long list of herbs popped up. Pictures of herbs and names and so much more. "Now, you tap on any of these names or pictures and the descriptions will come up for you."

She tapped on basil and so much information filled the screen. She began reading all about basil and some of the other things it was good for. Then she tapped on rosemary and read about rosemary. Before she knew it, Aidyn and the operatives had come home from the meeting and Shianne was gone. She didn't even hear her leave.

43

He finished his last bite of the pizza Lara had ordered and sat back. Tate was recounting the meeting.

"So Gerard, Kent, and Jasiah came down the mountain today. Craig refused. I guess he's in a bad state right now. No one can reason with him at all. But we came to some agreements. Those who want to, can come down the mountain and work. The town council will call a town meeting and talk to them about the truce. Special invitations will be sent out to everyone explaining that their input is vital. Fair wages will be paid, of course. The BRR people will have to get social security cards and receive payroll which also means they'll pay taxes. They'll also begin paying real estate taxes. How they handle that up there is their business. If they want their people to begin paying property taxes, they'll work it out. We suggested a one-time concession of wiping out the taxes that are currently due to the town of Glen Hollow. But, beginning immediately, they will incur real estate taxes. For their taxes, the town will begin bringing improvements up the mountain. Electricity and water first. It'll take time and we are all aware of it."

Aidyn watched Elena as Tate spoke. She asked, "What happens in the meantime?"

"Until the town council has met, and we all have an agreement, nothing. They do agree to only come down here on peaceful terms. If they want to begin looking for jobs, they can do that."

Grace nodded. "Most of them are peaceful. And if they can keep Craig under control, the rest will fall in line."

Lara asked, "What about last night? What will happen in regard to the shootings?"

Aidyn responded. "Nothing. Spencer and I were protecting ourselves. Ramsay and Brennen came here and shot up the house first. The fact that we followed them was in question as we became the aggressors, but we got Casper on the phone and he smoothed it over with the sheriff and the mayor. So no charges will be filed against Spencer or me and no charges will be filed against Ramsay and Brennen."

Grace laid her fork down quietly. "Are they still alive?"

Tate shrugged. "At the time of the meeting they were. We haven't heard otherwise since. We did offer to help them see the doctor down here. Kent said he'd speak with them."

Lara turned to Tate. "Is Kent sincere in helping solve all of this?"

"I believe he is. He apologized for the trouble he caused you. I told him he needed to apologize to you. But, between all of us, if he does, please give him a chance. It won't be easy for him to do."

"I understand."

Tate kissed Lara on the forehead, and he grinned.

The buzzer at the gate rang and Tate stood to answer it. He came back a few seconds later. "Everyone hang onto your hats, Shianne is back."

Lara grinned at Elena and he made a mental note to ask her how her afternoon had been.

Shianne burst through the front door and the rattle and crumpling of bags filled the air. "I could use some help." She called out and Lara went out to help her.

Henry stood. "I've got things to do."

Maya shook her head. "Chicken."

"Whatever."

Spencer stood. "I'm out of here too. Good luck ladies," he said to Elena and Grace, and Aidyn stood too.

Elena grabbed his arm. "No. You need to stay with me."

He chuckled. "I was just going to get a beer."

Spencer stopped. "I'll take one too."

"Tate?"

"Yeah. This is a beer kind of Saturday night."

Adelaide stood, "I'm pouring a glass of wine. I'll see if Maya wants one. Elena how about you? Grace?"

Elena looked at her mom, then Adelaide. "I've...we've never had wine."

"Mmm, okay then, let's do this. Besides," she thumbed over her shoulder, "You'll need it."

Adelaide left the room for a minute and Elena looked up at him. "What is it?"

"It's fermented grapes. You should only sip it. You can get drunk very fast on it. You're slight and never had it before, so it might hit you fast."

"Oh. Maybe I shouldn't..."

"I'll be here with you and you're safe here, sweetie."

He gave her a quick kiss then went to get everyone beers.

Shianne had the bags in the living room, and they made their way in there as she began pulling clothing out of bag after bag. Elena sat stiffly as Shianne first held up the various blouses and jeans and slacks for everyone to see, then piled them on either Elena's lap or Grace's. After all was unbagged, Shianne had three smaller shopping bags with handles and held them up. "These are unmentionables. I'll just set them here for you." And set two at Elena's feet and one at Grace's.

Elena looked into her bag and closed it quickly. Her cheeks turned the cutest shade of red and he grinned at her. She looked at him, embarrassment written on her face. "I didn't know what unmentionables were."

He winked at her. "You can show me later."

Her hands flew to her face, and he pulled her into his side and wrapped his arm around her shoulders.

"Finally." Shianne announced. "I got you each a dress. You may go out on the town some time or need it for a special occasion. These two are on me and from my shop."

She picked up two hangers with white plastic bags over them. Divine Designs was written on the bags. The first one was a pretty black dress with an embellishment around the neckline. She carried it to Grace. "I just know this will look stunning on you."

Grace's eyes filled with tears as she looked at the dress in her hands. She felt the material between her fingers and a small sob escaped her throat. "Oh, Shianne, this is simply stunning." Grace stood and hugged Shianne.

Shianne turned to Elena. "And Elena. This is for you. I got you a little black dress too, because every girl needs one."

"Really?"

"Yes. Really. This one is absolutely perfect for you."

She pulled the bag off the dress. The top was lace, the bottom a soft crepe material and he knew she'd look stunning in it. He'd have to find an occasion to take her out in it.

44

Elena hung her new clothing in the closet and tried not to think about the cost. The price tags were still on them all and she was stupefied by the numbers. First of all, she'd have to make a lot of money down here to just buy a shirt.

Aidyn had errands to run today. Tate and Lara were gone somewhere. Spencer and Adelaide were working and Henry and Maya, well she didn't know where they were.

She went to her mom's room and found her hanging her new clothes on hangars. "It's pretty overwhelming, isn't it?"

"That it is. But it's all starting to feel real."

"Good." She sat on the edge of the bed. "How are you feeling, Mama?"

"Better actually. Adelaide has me taking some vitamins and that's helping some. But I still get fatigued easily."

"That's understandable."

She played with the pattern on the comforter as her

mom continued hanging her clothing. "What's on your mind, Elena?"

"Mama, I don't want to brew with you. I don't mean with you because I don't love you. I mean, I don't want to brew the elixir anymore."

Her mom turned to her and sat down next to her. She reached over and took one of her hands and held it.

"I understand you don't mean me."

She huffed out a breath. "I want to grow herbs. But I've been reading in Lara's tablet that start-up costs can add up. Soil and plants. I have some seedlings and seeds, but likely not enough."

"I'll tell you what Elena. Let's talk about all of this after we get to Lynyrd Station and see what Dr. Nicholas thinks of the elixir. I'll help you however I can. I know Aidyn will too. He sure loves you."

"I love him too. But he's spent too much money on us already. Did you see the price tags?"

"I did. But I plan on paying him back. If the elixir doesn't bring in money, I can work once I'm better. We'll figure it out."

"Okay."

Her mom hugged her close and she closed her eyes and felt like a little girl again needing her mama's hug. Her mom whispered, "It's a lot of change right now. But we'll settle in."

"I know we will, Mama. I have to say, you're adjusting so much better than I am."

"Honey, I'm excited. I'm glad we aren't going to die up on that mountain. Your daddy and I wanted better for you. We just didn't know how to give it to you. Instead, you brought it to me. Your daddy would be so proud. I'm so proud of you. You were brave to go after what you wanted."

"I just wanted to be with Aidyn. I didn't want people getting shot or scared or maybe dead."

Her mom tucked her hair behind her ear. "Sometimes, when people are faced with big change, they fight it first. Craig was only bringing negative change up there and he would have made everyone miserable. I'll bet in ten years hardly anyone will live up on that mountain anymore. Just a few of the old timers."

"Yeah." She stood. "I think you're right, Mama." She stepped to the door. "I'm going to go outside and get some fresh air."

She walked through the house still marveling at the size of it. The massive amount of stuff they had in it staggered her. It made her feel uncomfortable, she'd always been fine with what she needed. All this other stuff was—stuff. It made life easier but, still, it was stuff.

She stepped through the garage. It was massive with so many vehicles gone. She heard music coming from a room at the far left and she moved toward it. Just as she was about to knock, Henry walked out. He was sweaty and huffing.

"Hey, Elena. Going to work out?"

"Work out? You mean go outside?"

He smiled at her and she thought he was handsome when he smiled. He didn't very often.

"This is our workout room." He opened the door for her and turned on the light.

It smelled sweaty and it was humid. There were mats on the floor and metal bars and circles laying around. She stared at it all not sure what she was looking at. When she looked at him he nodded and stepped inside. He pulled a bar with round things on the end off of a holder.

"These are weights. We lift them to build and tone muscle."

He lifted a few times and she understood what he was doing. He stepped over to a mat and took a rope off the wall. "This is a jump rope. It burns calories." He swung the rope over his head and jumped. After a few times he went very fast and she could hear him huff out a breath.

He stopped and grinned. "We do this several times a week to stay in shape."

"Oh." She touched some of the weights and the bars and nodded. "I see." She grinned. "I wasn't going to do this. I was going to take a walk outside."

He nodded. "I figured. But stay inside the gates until we know for sure it's safe. Okay? I don't want Aidyn mad at me if you get hurt."

"I will. Thank you."

She strode out the door and through the garage door and looked up at the sunshine. It was warm again today. It was unusually warm for January. She moved toward the picnic table and sat on it like Aidyn did. She stared at the mountain for a long time. She didn't miss it. She wondered how the people were, but if this whole group of people here promised to keep her safe if she went up there, she still wouldn't go. It had felt like a prison for the last few years. She'd dreamed of so much more but didn't know what that more was. Then she met Aidyn. He was her more. And, now it seemed like there was even more than she'd thought, and she struggled in her mind to know what to do and how to do it.

She looked down at her fingernails painted bright red. Her toes matched. Shianne had insisted on giving her a manicure and a pedicure last night, then made her mom do the same thing. Her nails had never looked prettier. She didn't know ladies painted their fingernails and toenails. She grinned as she saw them sparkle in the sunlight.

45
____

Aidyn entered the house and wandered around looking for everyone. It was quiet, which was unusual. He ambled to the bedroom and found Elena sitting in the armchair reading on Lara's tablet.

"Hey. What are you reading?"

"Herbs can grow under a thing called artificial light. They set up lights and fixtures and grow that way. But they don't taste the same as having natural sunshine. That's better. I think soil matters too. But it doesn't say that in here."

He laughed. "You're so damned cute."

She cocked her head to the side and furrowed her brows. "Why?"

He shook his head. "I don't know, you just are."

He sat at the foot of the bed and looked at her. Her legs tucked under her, her cute little painted toes, stuck out from under her. Her pretty fingers as they held the tablet. Her hair shined. She was stunning and he felt like the luckiest man on earth.

"Can I take you out and show you something?"

"Sure. Henry showed me your workout room. It smells in there."

He laughed. "It does smell. That's because we're always sweating in there. Tate's having a big fan installed next week."

"What is a fan and what will that do?"

He took her hand and pulled her to the garage while explaining a fan and its purpose. "Wait, you'll need shoes."

She ran back to the bedroom, her hair bouncing as she did. When she came back out, he admired her all over again.

He held his hand out to her and she smiled and clasped his hand. His heart thumped in his chest but it was a happy thump.

He helped her in his truck and moved them out of the HOG grounds and down the road.

"Where are we going?"

"Ah, well, I have something to show you. And it's very important."

"Is that what your errands were today?"

"Yes."

"Okay."

He drove to the parking lot where he used to park to wait for her.

"Do you know where this is?"

She looked at him, her brows furrowed. "Of course, I do. It's where you parked to meet me."

"Do you remember where we hid your basket?"

"I do." She pointed. "In the vines."

He played with the bracelet she'd made for him. He never took it off. He exited the truck and helped her out.

They walked hand in hand across the street to the vines at the bottom of the big tree.

"Reach in there."

She stared at him for a long time then stepped into the vines carefully and felt around for what she didn't know.

She pulled her hand up. "A basket!"

"Yep." He chuckled. "Open it."

She lifted the material he'd laid over it and there was a leather necklace he'd braided for her. She lifted it out and smiled. "Did you make this?"

"I did. It isn't as good as the bracelet you made me. But I never take this off and I wanted to make you something too. I intended to leave it for you the night we brought you down, but things happened and I didn't have time."

She slipped it over her neck and touched it with her fingers. "It's beautiful. Thank you."

He leaned in and kissed her. "There's more."

She felt around in the basket and pulled out the diamond ring he'd purchased for her today. She looked at it and turned it around in her hand, the sunlight made it sparkle.

He got down on one knee. "Elena Dorsey, will you marry me?"

Her eyes sought his and he saw the tears there. One spilled down her cheek before she answered and it took her a long time to say anything.

"Yes."

He took the ring from her hand and slid it on her finger. "We can have it sized tomorrow."

She looked at her finger with her sparkling diamond ring on it and tears flowed down her cheeks. She jumped into his arms and he squeezed her tightly to him.

"I will always remember this spot right here as my favorite place in the world, Aidyn. The anticipation of coming here to find notes from you or leaving notes for you made my entire day. This is the place you saved me. Right here."

He pulled his phone out and said, "Let's take a selfie."

"A what?"

He chuckled. "A picture." He pulled her close and snapped pictures. He took a picture of her ring and stepped back and took a picture of Elena with the basket in her hand and a ring on her finger and the most beautiful smile he'd ever seen.

"Let's go home and tell everyone."

"Okay." They got in the truck to leave, and she stared at the tree for a long time. "Can you take a picture from this spot too?"

"Sure." He took a picture and showed it to her.

"Is it possible to take a picture from above the place where the basket was? That was the view I always had."

"Elena. Honey, until things are safer, do you think it's wise to go up there on their land?"

Her lips turned up softly. "No. I guess not."

They drove home, but she held his hand and the sparkle that glowed from that ring filled the truck with colorful sparkles.

As they entered the kitchen, most everyone was there, sitting at the table or counter and talking.

"Hi."

Tate responded first. "Hi. Out and about today?"

"Kind of."

He looked down at Elena and she smiled up at him. He shrugged. "Show them."

She held up her hand and the room erupted. Hugs

and congratulations were offered from everyone. Grace hugged him hard. "You take care of my baby, Aidyn."

"I promise you on my life, Grace."

She squeezed him again and Lara announced that they needed a toast. He pulled bottles of wine from the wine fridge, and they filled glasses. They toasted to new beginnings.

Tate called him aside briefly. "Hey, before you walked in, we got word that Craig is being handled, but he isn't taking it well. He came down to the construction site and shot off a few rounds at the containers. He seemed drunk."

"Are Spencer and Adelaide alright?"

"They're fine. They went outside when he stopped and managed to get him disarmed. Kent came down the mountain and got him."

"Okay. I'm glad he didn't hurt anyone."

"Yeah. But let's celebrate you and Elena. We'll deal with everything else tomorrow."

EPILOGUE

Elena finished covering up the seeds she'd planted and watered them. Just enough. She swept up the soil that had fallen on the floor and put the broom away.

They'd bought a place just out of town, next to Aidyn's parents. The last year had been one of many changes. They'd moved to Lynyrd Station. Got married. Her mom decided she didn't want to actually brew the elixir every day, so she trained one of Chase's staff on how to do it. That was after they'd tested it and found it had many healing properties. Chase bought the recipe and training for the elixir for a wild amount of money and Elena built her greenhouses. She hadn't gotten a first crop from them yet, but it was getting close. Hopefully, before this little one was born.

She ran her hand over her burgeoning belly and rubbed her back as she waddled to the front of the greenhouse.

"Hey, there you are."

Aidyn stepped up to her and kissed her lips, then her

belly as he'd done every day, several times a day since she found out she was pregnant.

"My mom is looking for you."

"Okay." She waddled toward the door. "Is she here?"

"No, she's at their place."

"Why didn't she come here?"

"Honey, you've been at this for so many hours and I can see your back is hurting. Please let's go and see what she wants."

Though they were next door, the acreage between them made it an impossible walk today. Right now at least. But in the years ahead, she envisioned walking with the baby in its stroller to Grandma's house.

As they pulled into his parents' driveway there were a few other cars there. She looked down at her dirty jeans and shirt. "I'm dirty."

"So am I. Don't worry. I promise."

Her stomach twisted then the baby kicked and dug his toes into her ribs. She held her breath as Aidyn opened the door.

"Is he being naughty again?"

She let out her breath and nodded.

He kissed her tummy again. "Come on, buddy, give momma a break."

She laid her hand on his head and fluffed his hair. "He listens to you. That means I'm in trouble."

He grinned. "I'll save you." She smiled at him and he kissed her lips. "Let's go see my mama."

"Okay." She huffed out as she sat up.

They entered the house and a bunch of people jumped up and yelled, "Surprise."

She jumped back, but Aidyn was there to catch her. "It's a surprise baby shower." Bridget yelled. Then she noticed, everyone was dirty. They all had dirt on their clothes and faces.

"Why are you all dirty?"

Aidyn laughed. "Mom knew you were coming from the greenhouse and so we all got dirty."

She turned and looked at Aidyn's clothes, then everyone else's.

She started laughing. "That's funny. How did you all get dirty?"

Bridget led her to the sliding doors leading to the large wooden deck. "We all planted flowers for your greenhouse. You said you wanted to add mums, gerbera daisies, carnations, coneflowers, sunflowers, and petunias. We each planted a dozen of them so you have plenty to add to the greenhouse."

Her eyes welled with tears, though lately, her hormones had her crying often. But this was special.

"Thank you."

Bridget hugged her and patted her belly. She didn't allow many people to do that. What was it with everyone wanting to touch your belly when you were pregnant anyway? But Bridget and her mom were allowed.

She looked around at the faces milling about to celebrate their baby. Their friends from Kentucky weren't here, but their parents were. Tate's mother, Sophie, hugged her and playfully whispered, "I'm still waiting for my first grandchild."

She laughed. "I'll tell Lara to get busy."

She looked around for her mom and finally saw her near the big fireplace. Her mom waded through the crowd and wrapped her in a big hug.

Aidyn and Elena opened all the beautiful gifts from the people who had folded her into their families and helped Aidyn and her so much. She had built-in babysitters and what a dream that was for new parents.

She stood and stretched; her back had been bothering her so much lately. Aidyn slid his arms around her from behind and pulled her gently to his body. He kissed the side of her head. "Back hurt again?"

"Yeah."

He kissed her ear. "We can go home anytime you're ready."

That low ache intensified again and caught her breath short. She inhaled and let her breath out, then turned in his arms. "Actually, I think we need to head to the hospital. But first I need a shower."

He looked into her eyes and whispered, "Are you in labor?"

"Yeah. I've had low pains all day. I've managed to breathe through them, but this last one was harder."

"Elena!"

"Shh. Let's just go. Please."

Aidyn kept his arm around her as they slipped out.

As they pulled away from the house, the front door opened, the partygoers spilling out into the front yard looking for them.

Another pain gripped her, and she panted through it. "We'll need to make this quick, Aid."

He chuckled. "Is every new start going to begin with a quick getaway?"

***

Spencer ducked under a tree branch and continued running. He had to catch the shithead who just cut his wires at the construction site and take him in. The BRR had been quiet for the past couple of months. Now this. It always seemed they took two steps forward and one back.

And, it rankled that they always focused on his wiring. He'd rewired this entire construction site on at least two occasions over the past year.

He jumped over a downed log, then bent to dip under a lean-to roof in the back of the laundromat.

The dark head turned a corner and his heels beat the ground. He rounded the corner and saw the kid or man, or whoever, duck between Divine Designs and The Broken Barrel, the local bar, which furrowed his brows. Why the kid didn't run up the mountain confused him.

F ind out who Spencer is chasing in Rescuing Kenna.
You can find it in my shop at - https://www.pjfi ala.com/product/rescuing-kenna-eb/

Or the retailer of your choice - https://geni.us/Kenna

ALSO BY PJ FIALA

You can find all of my books at <u>https://pjfiala.com/books</u>

Romantic Suspense

Rolling Thunder Series

Moving to Love, Book 1

Moving to Hope, Book 2

Moving to Forever, Book 3

Moving to Desire, Book 4

Moving to You, Book 5

Moving On, Book 6

Rolling Thunder Boxset 1, Books 1-3

Rolling Thunder Boxset 2, Books 4-6

Military Romantic Suspense

Second Chances Series

Designing Samantha's Love, Book 1

Securing Kiera's Love, Book 2

Bluegrass Security Series

Heart Thief, Book One

Finish Line, Book Two

Lethal Love, Book Three

Wrenched Fate, Book Four

Lynyrd Station Protectors - Security

Finding His Fire Book One

Finding His Mark Book Two

Finding His Jewel Book Three

Finding His Match Book Four

Big 3 Security Boxset, Books 1-3

Lynyrd Station Protectors - GHOST

Defending Keirnan, GHOST Book One

Defending Sophie, GHOST Book Two

Defending Roxanne, GHOST Book Three

Defending Yvette, GHOST Book Four

Defending Bridget, GHOST Book Five

Defending Isabella, GHOST Book Six

GHOST Box Set One (Books 1-3)

GHOST Box Set Two (Books 4-6)

Lynyrd Station Protectors - RAPTOR

RAPTOR Rising - Prequel

Saving Shelby, RAPTOR Book One

Holding Hadleigh, RAPTOR Book Two

Craving Charlesia, RAPTOR Book Three

Promising Piper, RAPTOR Book Four

Missing Mia, RAPTOR Book Five

Believing Becca, RAPTOR Book Six

Keeping Kori, RAPTOR Book Seven

Healing Hope, RAPTOR Book Eight

Engaging Emersyn, RAPTOR Book Nine

RAPTOR Box Set 1

RAPTOR Box Set 2

RAPTOR Box Set 3

GHOST Legacy (Next generation)

Finding Lara, Book One

Saving Elena, Book Two

Rescuing Kenna, Book Three

Protecting Everleigh, Book Four

Guarding Adelaide, Book Five

Shielding Maya, Book Six

MEET PJ

Writing has been a desire my whole life. Once I found the courage to write, life changed for me in the most profound way. Bringing stories to readers that I'd enjoy reading and creating characters that are flawed, but lovable is such a joy.

When not writing, I'm with my family doing something fun. My husband, Gene, and I are bikers and enjoy riding to new locations, meeting new people and generally enjoying this fabulous country we live in.

I come from a family of veterans. My grandfather, father, brother, two sons, and one daughter-in-law are all veterans. Needless to say, I am proud to be an American and proud of the service my amazing family has given.

My online home is https://www.pjfiala.com.
You can connect with me on
Facebook: https://www.facebook.com/PJFialaAuthor
Instagram: https://www.Instagram.com/PJFiala.
YouTube: https://youtube.com/@PJFiala
TikTok: https://www.tiktok.com/@pjfiala?lang=en
If you prefer to email, go ahead, I'll respond - pjfiala@ pjfiala.com.

COPYRIGHT

9 781959 386391